Michael's Choice

Sequel to "The Gift"

Barbara Avon

Copyright © 2017 Barbara Avon

All rights reserved

No part of this book may be reproduced or transmitted in any form or by any means, electronic or mechanical, including photocopying, recording or by any information storage and retrieval system, without written permission from the author, except for the inclusion of brief quotations in a review. For permission requests, write to the publisher, at the E-mail address below to the attention of Barbara Avon:

Email: barbaraavonauthor@gmail.com

All of the characters in this book are fictitious and any resemblance to actual persons, living or dead, is purely coincidental.

Cover design by Barbara Avon

Acknowledgements

Writing is much like looking into a mirror and talking to yourself. Really, that's what it is. A writer is put on a path towards self-discovery and the journey is both terrifying and thrilling.

When I wrote "The Gift", part 1 to this book, I never intended to write a sequel. However, writing is also sharing of yourself, and my readers were intent to see more of Michael Rossi. I always listen to my readers. A line in this book reads as follows: "What's the point of art, if it hides?" The same concept applies to writing and giving the reader what the reader wants. In turn, they are gifting me something – the ability to share of myself and breathe new life into a character that ultimately, has become a part of me. I am forever indebted.

I would like to thank Susan Day (Author), who has played a role in guiding me on this journey. Because of her never-ending support, and because she helped me gain further exposure in that thing we call the internet. (What is the point of being an author if she hides?) My gratitude is endless. You can find "Enthralled Magazine" online.

To my family: my Father, Domenic, Brother, Jerry, beautiful Niece, Emma and my amazing Nephews, Nicholas, Nico and Matteo, and to my incredible Mamma who watches us from above: you give me life and I love you beyond words.

To my brother-in-law, John and my sister-in-law, Sonia: true family is not solely bound by blood, but by love.

To Danny, my husband. How incredible are you? You have been there for me, through thick and thin (and countless readings.) You've watched me tear my hair out and celebrated with me when I found "just" the right word. You are my everything, and I love you with all that I am, into infinity. P.S. Thank you for your ideas and input, my love.

Finally, this book is dedicated to my gorgeous sister, Linda: My life-long friend, and confidant; my keeper of secrets; fellow reader and lover of romance. You were my maid of honor and are the mother to my beautiful niece and nephew. I'm the older sister, but it is you, that I look up to. This book is for you.

One

October 5th, 1982

The living room was half in shadows. "Mood lighting", his girlfriend had called it. Tom Kaufman, football star, lady's man, and all-around nice guy, was walking around his parents' mansion trying to find some semblance of order among the throngs of people lighting up and drinking expensive liquor straight from Europe that his father brought back after every trip. His girlfriend had already left so she could wake up early in the morning and study. She wanted to be a veterinarian, and she was one step away from getting into her preferred school – the University just out of town, where her grandfather had attended and graduated with top honours.

A jock was passed out upstairs in the hallway that led to the bedrooms. Tom kicked at him to make sure the guy was still alive. He grunted in response.

In his parents' room, a massive area complete with a fireplace, skylight, and an ensuite with a bathtub that could fit three people, Donna Smith was sprawled across the bed, on her stomach. In a miserable attempt to hide, she left the lights off, and let the moonlight show her the way. Tom didn't have to see her to understand. The sniffing made it obvious.

"No drugs," he said, flicking the light switch.

Donna turned to her side, a rolled-up bill in her hand, and a mirror beneath her nose. "You're a terrible host, Tom Kaufman."

He walked over to her and pulled at her arm. "Raid daddy's stash, again? Come on, princess. Downstairs."

"Don't you want to kiss me first? I won't tell your

girlfriend." She attempted to look seductive by posing with one hand on her slim waist and the other pulling at the strap of her dress, exposing a white lacy bra.

Temptation sat on his left shoulder whispering obscenities in his ear. Donna had long blonde hair, and blue eyes – the perfect specimen according to his buddies. Her figure was the exact shape of the hourglass that sat on the fireplace mantel. Still, the remnants of white powder above her top lip turned him off, not to mention he was in love with someone else.

"Out. Party's over."

She blew him a kiss and left the room, following her downstairs where a couple was arguing in the expansive foyer.

"I want to go home!"

"Just another hour, babe."

"I'm tired."

"Look," he told her, pointing to the couch. "It's empty. Go sit, okay?"

She stomped her foot like a child but told him, "Fine. One more hour."

Tom walked over to his buddy. "Trouble in paradise?"

"I don't know why I bother except that the sex is hot as hell."

"That-a-boy," Tom told him sarcastically, clapping him on the shoulder.

"What? Don't tell me that you and…"

"My sex life is none of your business, so stop right there."

Tom turned away to answer a knock on the giant front door. He hoped it wasn't more of his peers seeking a good time. The house was already a disaster.

Donna walked up to him and placed her hands on one of his shoulders, her groin against his hip, claiming him for the night. What the girlfriend didn't know, wouldn't hurt her.

"Hey, Tommy," she said, smiling until all her teeth showed.

Tom sighed and pulled at the door. "Great. Who the hell ordered pizza?"

Donna played with the hair at the nape of Tom's neck. He swatted at her. "Knock it off, would you?" Turning to the pizza guy, he asked him, "How much?"

"$32.50"

"For four pies? Jesus... here's forty. Take the girl home," he said, cocking his head towards Donna, "and I'll give you another ten."

"Hey! I'm not leaving," she pouted, swaying on her feet.

"Yeah, you are. What do you say, buddy?" The pizza guy was eyeing the young blonde whose eyes were half-closed. "She only lives four blocks from here."

"It would be my pleasure to drive the young lady home."

"Great. Here's your fifty."

"You're going to pay for this, Tommy."

"I'm sure I will," he told her, helping her into her coat.

She shrugged it off and held it scrunched in her arms, pinched his backside, and before he could push her out the front door, she managed to kiss his lips, too.

"Nighty-night, Tommy."

She walked past both him and the pizza guy, and stood on the lawn, waiting.

"Thanks again, buddy. She's a little, uh, drunk."

"We gotta look out for each other. Enjoy the pizza."

Tom watched as the man opened the side door of his white car for the girl and helped her inside. She waved at him, and he lifted two fingers in a "V" before closing the front door with a bang.

In the car, the delivery man asked her, "Which way, Miss?"

"That way," she told him, pointing through the windshield, and giggling for no reason. Her legs were bare underneath her short, pink, Lycra dress.

The pizza guy swerved in the opposite direction.

"Hey! I said the *other*, that way."

"Just taking a short-cut."

"Oh."

She rolled down her window and stuck her head outside

like a dog, enjoying the fresh autumn air. The man stole glances at the silky white skin of her thighs like a butcher does a fresh cut of meat. He drove down the streets of the residential neighbourhood, taking a left that entered a wooded area. The dirt road underneath the tires alerted the girl.

"Never been on this short-cut," she told him, growing frazzled, and sitting back in her seat.

"It's quicker. What's your name?"

"Donna."

"Nice to meet you, Donna. That boy wasn't very nice to you, was he?"

"Tommy's a jerk!" she said, animated. "A rich jerk, but still a jerk."

The man was unimpressed. The boy was doing her a favour and she was disrespecting him. She played with the buttons on the radio trying to find a good song.

"Did I tell you that you could touch my radio?"

"What?"

"Did I give you *permission?*"

She merely laughed and kept her hand on the dial. Slamming on the brakes and putting the car in park, the man grabbed her wrist and squeezed hard.

"Owww!"

"Hurts, doesn't it?"

"Let me go!"

"I have a better idea," he said, opening his door and walking around her side of the car.

"Come on, now. Get out," he told her through the window.

"Why?"

"Get *out!*"

She did as she was told and looked around her, seeing nothing but forest. The man grabbed at her wrist and pulled her behind him like a parent would a spoiled child, leaves crunching underneath their feet as he dragged her into an area that was thick with trees.

"Where are we *going?*"

"Quiet, now."

Tears flooded her eyes, and she was suddenly sober as she came to the realization that she was in trouble.

"I'm sorry I touched your radio."

"Not good enough," he told her, still dragging her behind him.

"*Please.*"

"Begging is un-lady like." He stopped abruptly and faced her, still grasping her wrist. "And so is this dress," he said. He took the switchblade from his back pocket and flicked it open. Grabbing the material of the dress where it met her thighs, he sliced upwards until it hung open like an unbuttoned coat.

Donna screamed and covered herself with her arms; crossing her legs against the night air, and the man who could clearly see she wasn't wearing underwear tonight – to seduce Tommy.

"Suddenly shy, you little slut?" he pulled at the straps of her dress, releasing her arms from it so that he was free to grasp her bra and he removed it like one would a sweater, over her head.

"Please, *stop!*"

"That's what they all say. Lie down."

"No...!"

He sighed and pushed her down, placing his foot on her chest, between her breasts. She couldn't move from the weight of his body on hers and she struggled fruitlessly. Her head writhed back and forth, her hands on his ankle. He bent over, as if tying his shoelace, and sliced at her throat, giving her a bloody necklace.

"Finally, peace and quiet."

Working diligently, he turned her over and admired her naked body, young and fresh, and marked the girl on her pink thighs by sliding his knife down her legs, and over her calves so that it looked like she was wearing stockings.

"That's more appropriate for a young lady, eh?"

An animal moved in the tree nearby and the man greeted

it kindly, "Hello little creature. Sorry for the intrusion. I'll be gone soon."

He turned the girl over so that her lifeless eyes faced the stars. They were very pretty eyes and he almost felt bad for taking one of them. The squish of the knife blade against human flesh and bone was like music to his ears.

"Next time, *Donna*, you must ask for permission before you touch someone's property."

He walked swiftly back to his car, opened the trunk, and pulled out a shovel. He was hungry and made a mental note to stop at the *Dairy Queen* on his way home. Making his way back, the squirrel in the tree his only witness, he quietly sang an old tune in her memory:

<blockquote>
I had a girl
Donna was her name
Since she left me
I've never been the same
'Cause I love my girl
Donna, where can you be?
</blockquote>

Two

November 1982

His hand was over her mouth. She could barely breathe and fought to suck in air. His body was almost crushing her as he hovered over her. She was cloaked in a darkness so black; it was like an oil slick. Sweat trickled down his naked back and he radiated a heat that served to shield them from the wintry air that penetrated their bedroom window. She couldn't stifle the sounds that escaped her throat, calling out in release.

"Shh! You're going to wake Maria, baby."

She pushed him off her and mounted him, causing her long dark hair to fall over his face. Her eyes closed, she loved him like no other time, until his fingernails dug into her hips, and he raised his own hips to dance with the woman he loved. Music was unnecessary.

She turned to look at the baby monitor on her nightstand, as it blinked rhythmically in the darkness, mimicking the rhythm of her body against his. Her voice drifted down to him, "The baby's fine."

The century old tree outside their window waved at them as it swayed in the fierce wind. Winter had arrived early in Ottawa this year, causing the city to shut down when it should have been alive this Saturday night.

It was only seven at night, and they chose to take advantage of the time between naps, feedings, and diaper changes – their dinner turning cold on the stove top.

Michael had instructed Mo to close the pizzeria and send staff home with whatever they desired from the kitchen. He was not the type of man to re-heat the day's menu items and serve them as *The Special* the following day. The day he allowed himself to do that, would be the day his soul died.

He felt her face against his neck, her breath warm on his skin, and he turned to kiss her hair and whisper the words that have been present on his lips for almost two years, "I love you."

It was then that they felt each other's release like an internal earthquake, penetrating walls that would never crumble, and as their bodies trembled, still united, she fell into him, giggling, and crying, at the same time. His lips stayed in her hair as he tried to labour his breathing until finally, she rolled off him and lied next to him staring at the ceiling. He turned to his side and brushed his fingertips over her body, running the length of her torso, her arms, and her thighs, stopping, in the end, on her mouth, where his touch lingered, trying to produce sound where there was none.

"What are you thinking?"

He sensed her turning her head to look at him, although it was too dark to see. He imagined the rosiness in her cheeks and the look in her eyes, when she answered, "That I love you too."

She sat on the edge of the bed and found her clothes that lay on the cold floor, discarded in a moment of passion.

"Where are you going?"

"To check on the baby."

"Hurry."

He swatted at her backside, but he missed.

When she was gone, Michael turned on his bedside lamp and pulled a smoke from the package. He lit the cigarette and stared at the wedding ring he's worn for a year and a half, cursing at the fact that it was on the wrong finger. The scars that covered half his body forced him to wear his ring on his good hand. Somehow, he felt the shiny gold looked dull in comparison to how it would look if he could wear the symbol of his love for her on the proper hand.

He still choked on bile when he thought of him. He still choked, revisiting the scenario as it played out in his head. An oblivious Phelps was impaled against the plastic horn of the carousel unicorn as Michael lied in the snow, trying to extinguish the flames that engulfed him. In his vision, the one he imagined, it was him, and not Nicole who put an end to Stevie Phelps' life. He's never admitted this to his wife. He has never dared to even speak of Stevie to the woman who suffered at his hand. Instead, Michael relished the would-be scenario in solitude. He imagined his hands around Stevie's throat and imagined looking on with pleasure as his eyes bulged from their sockets. Michael's scars are a constant reminder of that day at *Hayden's Amusement Park*, and although he has sworn to Nicole that he is not ashamed of his scars, the truth is, he would love nothing more than to turn back the hands of time and once again, be face to face with Ottawa's first serial killer. Time, however, is much like a dream. It flows and ebbs through us and nothing could ever alter it. Like a dream, it is what it is.

Michael crushed out his cigarette and pulled his sweatpants over his legs. He stopped in front of the dresser mirror where he studied his body. In some places, his skin was shrivelled like peeling wallpaper. His own reflection looked foreign to him but despite what he deemed imperfections, he was still met with stares from women, and young girls, and their gaze had nothing to do with his scars. He was simply more ruggedly handsome, Nicole had told him one day.

He walked down the hallway and stood at the threshold of his daughter's room where both his ladies were oblivious to his presence. Nicole was feeding the baby and he watched her as she sat in the rocker next to the crib. He crossed his arms over the defined muscles of his chest, with one hand on the opposite elbow, as if mimicking his wife by holding an invisible baby. Maria had just turned eight months old, and as he stood there, half-naked, admiring the scene before him, he remembered the day of her birth on an icy February afternoon:

Michael was pacing the hospital corridor as sympathetic staff looked on.

"He's going to put a dent in the floor," said one plump female

nurse to her colleague.

"Uh-oh, I think he heard you."

Michael walked up to the nurse's station for the hundredth time, "Goddammit, isn't there any news yet!?"

His eyes were as wild as his dishevelled hair. Caffeine ran through his veins. The sweater he wore felt suffocating and he pulled it over his head to reveal the scars on his left arm.

"Calm down, Mr. Rossi."

"You calm down," he replied nonsensically, pounding one fist on the counter.

The young nurse looked at him with understanding but her colleague, an older woman with years of experience, had little patience for the man who was disturbing the other patients and their families in the waiting room.

"Calm down, or I will call security."

Unaware of who she was speaking with, she considered the matter closed. His wife was admitted four hours earlier and the baby would make its appearance when it was ready. Michael, however, stayed true to his Italian temper and raised his other hand to put both fists on the counter, the sweater crumpled beneath them.

"Go ahead."

"Excuse me?"

"I said, go ahead and call security."

Just as the nurse was about to pick up her phone, a young doctor approached them.

"You can come in now, Mr. Rossi."

"It's about damn time!"

The doctor shrugged at the nurses and followed the new father down the hallway who was looking left and right, oblivious to the old man with the walker, and the teen boy in a wheelchair with his leg in a cast.

"Where are they?"

"This way."

They made a turn around a corner, and just as the doctor thought that Michael would raise his voice once more, he was shocked to feel the man's hands in his own.

"Thank you, Doc. Thank you," Michael said tearfully, shaking the doctor's hands with vigour. He thrust his sweater at him, and the doctor stared at it, unsure of what to do with it.

"Uh…you're welcome," he stated, pushing open the door to Nicole's hospital room. Michael stood at the doorway, unable to move.

"Hey, honey…"

He looked at his wife as if she were an artifact enclosed in protective glass in a museum. She held something in her arms, wrapped in pink.

"It's a girl."

He stood frozen in place. His t-shirt was already damp from sweat.

"Michael?"

Finally, as if shoved from behind, he made his way to the side of Nicole's bed. Without looking at the bundle in his wife's arms, he kissed Nicole on the forehead.

"Are you okay, baby?"

"Tired, but yes, I feel amazing. Want to hold her?" She pushed the baby towards Michael who looked away and studied a medical poster on the wall.

"What's wrong?"

"I…I'm afraid," he admitted, clutching at the sheet on the bed. "Okay? I don't think I can."

With the love and patience that she was known for, Nicole put two fingers on the side of Michael's face, guiding his eyes downward.

"Look," she told him. "It's your daughter. There's nothing to be afraid of."

His eyes were squeezed shut.

"Open your eyes, honey."

They stayed closed.

Nicole cleared her throat, feeling her patience wane, "Michael. Open. Your. Eyes."

Finally, Michael cocked one eye open, and a blurry outline of a tiny human came into focus. He opened his other eye, and from *that moment on, he was doomed. He was doomed to forever live his life without his heart, because his daughter now held it in her hands.*

It was Nicole who suggested they name her after Michael's mother who had died ten years earlier, and Maria Rossi became the entity that would forever define him as something new. He was a father, and it was a title that he coveted.

Afterwards, he sent the nurses at the hospital, a large pepperoni pizza along with a thank-you card: Sorry for being an ass, *he wrote.*

Nicole looked up to see her husband standing in the doorway. She put one finger to her nose before he could speak. She set the baby back in her crib and made her way over to Michael who took one of her arms and swung her against the wall in the hallway. He pressed his body against hers, one knee between her thighs, and raised her hands over her head. He found her mouth and quieted her by trapping her tongue, tasting her, and gently teasing her, until she realized that if his love was like an earthquake, she needed to prepare herself for the aftershock.

Three

"What are you doing?"

Michael stared at his watch, conscious of the fact that he needed to be at the restaurant. Mario, Michael's head chef, was already seething that Curtis had called in sick. The kid had a show at 11:00 am. He attracted much of the younger crowd, wowing them with his pizza flipping, a self-taught skill that had earned Curtis admirers from both the patrons, and the staff at *Michael's Place.* The lost revenue from today's cancelled show sent Mario in a frenzy. He'd also have to work doubly hard during the lunch rush, and Mario proclaimed more than once a day that he was getting too old to run in circles.

"Maybe you should lay off the pizza," Michael had told him, once.

"Maybe you should shut up," Mario had replied, unamused.

Michael had already finished a large cup of coffee and the interview was going nowhere. He had agreed to meet Eric Summers when he called him at the restaurant under the pretense of writing a story about *Michael's Place,* but so far, the topic at hand had nothing to do with Italian cuisine.

Eric Summers wrote for *The Herald*, Ottawa's leading newspaper. In the Spring of the previous year, Summers had taken an award-winning picture of the carousel at *Hayden Park.* Despite the fine he paid for trespassing at the crime scene, his photo, "Portrait of a Serial Killer", went national.

Summers shifted towards the man before him. A waitress walking by had distracted him. She had the shape of a belly dancer, and the moves, too.

"What?"

"Look, kid, are we going to get to it, or are you going to scope out women all day? I don't have time for this bullshit." Michael's face was turning different shades of red, causing Eric to fidget with the note pad in front of him. He knew that flattery wouldn't work on a man like Michael Rossi, so he decided to just cut to the chase.

"Like I said earlier," he stated, trying to dislodge the frog in his throat. "I appreciate you meeting with me."

"Got it. And?"

"And as you might know, I've acquired a certain level of prestige in the past year."

"Hadn't a clue," Michael replied honestly, crushing his cup underneath one hand.

"Oh, well, it's true. I know about your other skill, Mr. Rossi. I know about your photography."

Despite Michael's efforts to give the kid a second chance, he considered the interview over and stood from his chair causing other diners to notice the six-foot tall man who filled out his jeans in all the right places.

"I don't know what my photography has to do with anything but thanks for wasting my time, kid. You can lose my phone number."

"Wait!"

Desperate to keep Michael at the table, Eric reverted to Plan A. "I know you're very good. Your pictures, I mean. You have a talent. Please, give me five more minutes."

Michael looked around the breakfast diner, sighed from somewhere deep in his lungs, and sat back down. He guessed that the kid had seen his work up at the restaurant. Nicole had hung several pictures up at the pizzeria, stating, *"What's the point of art if it hides?"*

He stared at Summers, who donned a fedora and a pencil behind his ear like he was living in the wrong era.

"Five."

"Thank you," Eric expelled, along with his breath. He almost apologized for his next words, but he spat them out. "I'm writing a book, Mr. Rossi. About Stevie Phelps."

The colour in Michael's cheeks washed away instantly. A pit in the hollow of his belly inflated in seconds, making him want to vomit.

"What did you say?"

"I'm writing a book…a bio of sorts, and I want to include pictures. I was hoping that maybe I can use some of yours. The ones of your wife. She's a celebrity, you know…"

"A celebrity."

"Yeah."

Michael sat motionless, teeth clenched underneath his five o'clock shadow.

"I'll give you the credit you deserve, of course. A mention in the acknowledgements. You'll keep your own copyright but all royalties from potential sales of the book will remain with me."

Michael moved his head, and pushed it toward Summers like a dinosaur might have just before devouring his prey.

"Credit, eh?"

Summers shifted nervously in his chair and lit a smoke, dropping the match to the floor.

"Uh, yeah. I mean, I guess I can consider putting your name on the front cover. It would depend on what my publisher recommends, of course."

"Of course," Michael stated flatly, sitting back in his chair and stuffing one hand in his pocket. "Where did this…interest… for Phelps come from?"

"Well, like I was saying," Eric stammered, puffing away. "I took a picture last Spring that garnered quite a bit of attention. Maybe you've heard of it? *Portrait of a Serial Killer?*"

The memory was clear. Michael had been engrossed in the crossword as he was every day, and the picture occupied the entire front page of *The Herald*: The words *73 and countin'* were captured in hazy shades of green where the text was scratched into the metal of the carousel. Authorities were dumbfounded and speculators surmised that it had to have been a joke:

Stevie's last laugh. There was no way that one man, not even a psychopath, could kill so many. Michael had torn the front page off the newspaper and burned it underneath a match in the kitchen sink but of course, Nicole saw the paper as it sat in every store front, and every box in the city. He discarded his attempts at finishing the crossword that day. Every word he tried to enter materialized as D.E.A.T.H.

Summers had extinguished his smoke and was staring at his doughnut, but he didn't take a bite. He was aware of the man in front of him who was scrutinizing him through the slits in his eyes.

"So, what do you think?"

The smirk on Michael's face dissolved and he didn't try to keep his voice down. Like his signature trademark, his voice grew a decibel louder whenever he was aggravated or even happy. Basically, Michael was always loud.

"I think you're a sick bastard, and if you ever try to contact me again, there might be seventy-four murders in this city by the end of the year."

Michael pushed back in his chair so that the legs scraping against the floor sounded like nails on a chalkboard. Before turning to leave, he added, "I think you should change vocations, kid. Maybe something in deep sea, would suit you better."

Eric sat unflinchingly, unwilling to show Michael the depth of his insecurities. "Why do you say that?"

"You give photographers a bad name. You belong with the other sharks. Don't forget to pay my bill."

When he was gone, Eric motioned for the waitress, the one with the curves that could out-match *The Birth of Venus* in a wet t-shirt contest.

"More coffee?"

"I'm good, thanks. Do you have a phone book?"

"Sure thing."

"And the bill, please."

When she returned with the bill and the phone book, Summers left exactly $3.53 on the table and opened the thick book to somewhere near the end. He scrolled under "P" for "Publishers". Taking the pencil from behind his ear, he wrote the name and number on the back of the bill. He wasn't done with Michael – not yet. Flipping a few pages more, he found M & N Rossi on Regent Street in Downtown Ottawa. He's always wanted to meet a celebrity.

Four

Detective Sam Valetti sat at home in his red checkered lazy-boy, a manila folder on his lap. He had fallen asleep while reviewing a case. Elise was in the kitchen making her famous Sunday roast beef, oblivious that her husband was snoring away.

After forty years on the force, Valetti was close to retirement. His wife had given up trying to get him to retire early. The Phelps case had aged him beyond his years, and she worried about him. Often, she would hear him speak his dreams at night, and the story was never pretty. Just recently, she had to nudge him for a good ten minutes before successfully quieting him. He was talking to someone out loud, telling them to *hide the blood*. The dream didn't make sense, and he didn't remember a thing about it in the morning. He simply kissed her and told her that she worried too much.

She walked to the living room, still holding a ladle in one hand. They've been married thirty-five years and she still saw the young man standing proud in his officer's uniform, eager to impress. They were married before the accident, the one that would claim one of his eyes. The patch he wore over one eye did not eclipse the kindness that shone through. She still remembered the day that the captain had called her. A young bride, she was still trying to perfect her new husband's favourite, spaghetti, and meatballs, and with her hands full of ground meat, she answered the phone reluctantly, cursing a little beneath her breath.

When she learned that Sam was at the hospital, a surge of electricity pulsed through her entire body.

"Is he all right!?"

"They had to take his eye, Elise. But he'll be fine."

Elise wondered how *fine* someone could be when faced with the knowledge that they would have to get used to living with only one eye, and she wanted to tell the captain that very thing. Instead, she sped through town and arrived at the hospital exactly twenty minutes later.

When the Stevie Phelps murders shocked the city, Sam Valetti took up temporary residence at the precinct sleeping on a small couch he turned into a make-shift bed. He was rarely home, determined to unravel the mystery surrounding the murders.

Elise wondered if Sam's obsession with the case had do to with the fact that Phelps often extracted the victim's eyes, like her husband was seeking vindication for the victims simply because he could empathize with them.

She watched him as he stirred, but he was quiet, and she decided to let him sleep. She kissed him gently on the cheek and retreated to the kitchen to peel potatoes that she would bake alongside the roast. Butter was the key, her mother had always told her, *"Be sure to coat your pan in butter."*

She opened the refrigerator and stuck her head inside searching for the butter that had made its way to the back of the fridge. When she emerged, she almost had a heart attack to find Sam standing next to her.

"Goodness, Sam, you startled me! I thought you were sleeping."

"I was," he said, taking the butter from her hands and placing it on the counter. He took his wife in his arms and kissed her thin lips.

"What was that for?" she asked him, catching her breath.

"Because I love you."

"I love you too."

He didn't tell her. He wanted to, but he didn't tell her that his dreams woke him. Somewhere, in the middle of a dark and empty street, he was talking to someone who was missing not one eye, but two.

"You're next," they promised him.

Five

"How did the interview go?"

"Don't ask."

"That good, eh?"

At *Michael's Place*, Jacob was behind the bar counting bottles in the beer fridge. The two men had met in November of 1980 when Michael had taken up permanent residence at a bar stool at the dive where Jacob used to work as a bartender. At the time, Michael was newly single and he found *Mort's* to be the perfect place to exorcise thoughts of his ex-girlfriend from his troubled mind. When Jacob offered a very drunk Michael a ride home, their friendship took off, and by Christmas, Mike had offered Jacob a job so that he didn't have to drive out of town each day. Coincidentally, *Mort's* closed its doors for good three weeks later.

"What happened?"

Michael sat at the bar and looked his friend in the eye. "I thought I told you not to ask me?"

"Yeah, but you know me, buddy. I'm like Kim at her gossip parties that she likes to call Tupperware parties. Fill me in."

Michael pulled a pack of smokes from his jeans and lit a cigarette. The lunch crowd was starting to pile in. Mike would be cooking in the kitchen, but first, he asked Jacob for an espresso.

When Jacob returned with the shot, he placed a bottle of Sambuca in front of his boss who poured a generous amount into his coffee, swung his head back, and gratefully felt the concoction slide down his parched throat.

"The asshole wasn't there to learn about the restaurant."

"What did he want, then?"

"Something he'll never get."

Michael thought about the jerk's request. He wanted pictures of Nicole because, apparently, she was a celebrity. People like Eric Summers sickened him. Those who take advantage of another person's misfortune, whether they are out for personal gain, or something more sinister, are the worst type of people and he was sure that it's true what they say: *the devil walks among us.*

"And that is…?"

"Look, kid. I gotta get to work. Have a good shift." "That's it? That's all I get?"

Michael walked away, and raised one hand without turning back, as if to say, *I'm done with this conversation.*

"*I might as well start attending Tupperware parties,*" Jacob mumbled under his breath.

~

"Are you an idiot? Or what?"

"*Hey!*"

Mario was belittling one of Michael's newest employees – an aspiring young chef with four mouths to feed. At the sound of his boss's voice booming behind him, Mario spun around to come face to face with Michael's chest, and took a step backwards.

"He used vegetable oil in the tomato sauce."

"I don't care if he put cayenne in it too, you will not speak to my staff that way."

Mario shook his head and walked away, cursing liberally.

Justin, the new employee, stood off to the side looking like he was about to run. "Sorry, Mike, my old boss told me to do it… to save money. I wasn't thinking. I'm sorry."

"Calm down, kid. No harm done. Just remember to use olive oil next time."

"No harm done?" Mario was unable to keep his mouth shut, and he spoke from the appetizer station.

"That's what I *said*. Where's Rick?"

"In the walk-in fridge…" Mario mumbled, staring at his cutting board.

Mike made his way to the back of the kitchen, patting Justin on the shoulder on his way. He's known Mario for twenty years. Michael's father had hired him when Peter Rossi still owned the pizzeria. The guy was as uncouth as they come, but Mike had promised his father that when the restaurant changed hands, no one would lose their job.

Mario hadn't always been a brute. Mike knew the exact moment he changed. Mario and his wife had been on vacation in Italy with their young son, and daughter. They were at the beach, enjoying family time, and the warmth of the Italian sun on their faces. Unexpectedly, the weather changed, and a relentless downpour made the beachgoers run. In the middle of everything, no one noticed when Mario's daughter, Elizabeth, was trampled by an unforgiving crowd. She suffered a broken nose that would forever change her appearance and from that moment forward, Mario's disdain for people manifested itself in every waking hour. Michael almost couldn't blame him. How a group of adults could be so careless was beyond his comprehension. There were moments, too, when the old Mario would emerge; the happy-go-lucky, kind man who liked to share food, and wine with his friends, but those moments were fleeting.

At the walk-in-fridge, Mike pulled at the door that was to remain slightly open at all times when occupied by an employee. The latch on the inside was temperamental and one night, Mike had locked himself in. Mo, his bartender, let him out when he realized that Mike had been gone for too long when he set off to retrieve mint for the Mojito recipe he was experimenting with. The only reason Mike hadn't replaced the door yet, was because he made another promise to his father and that was to retain the original integrity of the building. He was allowed to redecorate, but Pete wanted the original fixtures to remain as a sort of homage to all the years he put into erecting the business. Michael had put a sign on the door, in big, bold, letters: KEEP

OPEN IF YOU'RE INSIDE.

"Jesus Christ, are you kidding me?"

Rick was sitting on an upside-down milk crate chugging from a bottle of red wine. As soon as he saw his boss, he hid the bottle partially behind the crate, stood, and wiped the drink from his lips, but no amount of rubbing would erase the evidence of an open bottle at his feet. Besides, Mike had already seen him.

"I...sorry, boss."

"It isn't even bloody noon yet! Not to mention you know you can't drink on the job."

Rick was a short man in his late twenties. He's worked at *Michael's Place* for six months and he was always on time, worked hard, and never caused Michael any trouble, until today.

"What gives?"

An embarrassed Rick lifted his apron and started to pile onions in it. He answered Michael without looking at him, "Just releasing some steam, Mike."

"Stop. Stop what you're doing."

Rick froze and clutched the pile of onions to his body.

"What do you mean, by *releasing some steam*? Is the job too much for you?"

"*No!* I mean, no, of course not."

Michael didn't believe him. He often came in looking like he had just gone twelve rounds in the ring.

"Come on."

"Where are we going?" Rick asked him, worriedly.

"My office."

~

"Want a smoke?"

"Yeah, thanks."

Michael pushed his cigarettes across his desk, along with a glass ashtray, and waited while his employee lit a cigarette.

"What's going on?"

The fluorescent bulb in the ceiling flickered begging to be

replaced. Mike turned on his desk lamp and studied the shadows it cast over his desk. His artistic eye was always seeking new things to photograph and the lines that covered the desk, put there by the glow of the bulb against the tray of his metal inbox, reminded Mike of the bars of a prison cell. Prison, where Stevie would be if he lived. Phelps was still on Mike's mind and as if being punished, it was Michael who felt locked away – in the confines of his own mind. It's the innocent who often suffer a curse: that of remembrance.

"It's money, Mike," Rick told him between drags of his smoke, causing Michael to pay attention. "I'm going out of my mind."

Money. *The root of all evil*, Michael's father used to say. He quickly leafed through his mental filing cabinet and remembered Rick's wage.

"I'm not paying you enough?"

"Hell no. I mean, no, it's not that. I need this job. Please don't fire me."

Michael sat back in his leather chair and took a good look at the man before him. Rick's fingers were trembling beneath his smoke. His hair was greying at the temples, and the wrinkles around his eyes were too deep for a man in his twenties.

"No one's getting fired. What's the problem, though?"

Ashamed, Rick decided to tell his boss the truth. "I owe a bunch of money. I can't make the payments. I sold everything, and I *still* can't make the payments."

"Owe money to who?"

"A loan shark," he admitted.

The office phone rang. Michael picked it up, hearing Jacob on the other end tell him that he was out of orange juice for the mixed drinks. "Yeah, I'll get you a new case in ten minutes, thanks."

He put the phone back on the hook and turned back to Rick, urging him to continue.

"When my Susie got pregnant," Rick said with love in his eyes, "we hadn't planned on it. We were waiting to start a family, until we could get on our feet." He helped himself to another cigarette.

"Did you have the baby?"

"Yeah," Rick told him, unable to control the smile that invaded his lips whenever he thought of his son.

"Boy or girl?"

"A boy. Jesse."

Michael thought of Maria, and he longed to hold her. Nicole had taken her to the doctor's today for a check-up and he wondered if they were home yet. They were calling for freezing rain which always worried Michael whenever Nic had to drive in it.

"Anyway," Rick continued, "I thought I could pay him back, but each time a payment was due, something came up. First, the *damn* brakes on my car needed replacing. Then, the water heater broke, and now he's...never mind."

"He's...what?"

"Threatening us. I can't sleep at night. Every time I hear a sound outside in the yard, I think it's some goon or something. I can't take it, Mike!"

Michael was remembering when he was a teen, and the restaurant wasn't doing well. His mom and pop would stay up all night, going through the books and discussing where it was that they could cut corners. Mike rode the same bicycle for five years and even though he had outgrown it, there was no other choice. He knew what money troubles were, and he felt sorry for Rick and finally understood why he came to work looking like a living zombie.

Michael stood and walked across the room. Rick watched and mistakenly believed that Michael was about to open his door, and despite what he promised, fire him for being stupid enough to even approach a loan shark.

"I'm not going, Mike!"

Michael turned, confused. "What?"

"I'm not going, *goddammit!*"

"What are you talking about? Relax!"

Behind a black and white photograph Michael had taken of a landscape scene, he opened a safe, and walked back to his chair with a black bag in his hands.

"How much do you owe?"

Shocked, Rick was unable to speak.

"Well, kid? We don't have all day."

"I...uh...a grand."

Michael unzipped the bag and counted out fifteen, one hundred-dollar bills and pushed them across his desk at the man whose jaw wouldn't close.

"I can't take that."

"Get rid of the guy. Get some sleep, and put the rest away for Jesse."

"Jesus..." Rick sat with his head in his hands, literally praising God...and Mike.

"Get a hold of yourself. It'll be okay."

"How will I repay you?" Rick asked, raising his head.

"Don't be stupid. If you're still in debt with me, I really didn't do you any favours, did I? Just quit drinking in the walk-in-fridge."

Rick stood abruptly and thrust his chest out, along with his hand. "Thank you, Mike."

"I have one request," he said, taking his employee's hand.

"Name it. I'll do anything."

"I want you to go the Mission this weekend. Help them with lunch for the homeless."

Rick wasn't sure he heard him right. "You want me to do what?"

"Help at the Mission. A good deed."

"I...guess I can do that..."

"Good. Let's get back to work."

"Why?"

"Why, what?"

"Why'd you help me?"

"Selfish reasons. I can't afford for you to get knocked off. I need you here."

Rick cocked an eyebrow at him.

"I'm kidding. I know what it's like to be hungry," he admitted.
"If you ever do something so stupid again, I'll beat the hell out of you."

"Got it," Rick told him as soon as his breathing returned to normal. "Never again. I promise, Mike."

He left the room and Michael shook his head after him. He wished his father was alive. If he were, he'd tell him, *"Money may be the root of all evil, pop, but it sure as hell helps to have it sometimes."*

To pay off the devil, himself.

Six

"Daddy's home!"

Michael threw his keys on the three-legged table that sat near the stairwell. He left Jacob and Mo in charge and made his way home immediately after dinner service, careful to take it slow on the slick city streets. The freezing rain had started and although they lived only blocks from the restaurant, he needed his car today to be able to bring five cases of wine with him.

Maria cooed from her highchair, and he kissed the top of her dark head of hair first. Then he embraced his wife, kissing her and squeezing her ass.

"Jesus, I missed you both so much."

"I can tell," Nicole laughed, a Christmas ornament still in one hand.

"The tree? Already? It's November."

"It's the *end* of November, and yes, already."

She followed Mike to the kitchen where he opened the fridge and pulled out a beer.

"Want one?"

"No thanks."

Michael drank from the bottle, thirsty as hell. Nicole watched him with one hip against the threshold of the doorway.

"What did the doctor say?"

"Everything's fine."

"That's what he said?"

Nic sighed and made her way over to her husband, hugging him around the waist.

"She's a little light. She should weigh more by this age and before you start with me, Michael Rossi, I promise you that it's nothing to worry about."

Michael looked behind her to peek at the baby who was playing with a plush Santa.

"Are you su...."

"Yes, I'm sure!" she told him quickly, kissing him. "Are you hungry? I have a pasta bake in the oven."

"Not yet."

She expelled another long breath, but she didn't press the subject. When it came to his daughter, no amount of reassurance would help Michael to stop worrying. Changing her mind, she went to the fridge and found her own beer and opened it using the bottle opener that doubled as a fridge magnet. They bought the souvenir on their honeymoon where they sat around lazily for two weeks at a resort in Mexico. It was the first time that Nicole had ever flown in an airplane and when the plane touched down, she had gotten on her knees and kissed the ground beneath her.

"The roads were pretty bad, eh?"

"Yeah."

"It's supposed to continue all night."

"Uh-huh."

"I bought a Mercedes today."

"Cool."

"Michael!"

Her stern tone shook him out of his thoughts. "What?"

"You know damn well, what. She is *fine!*"

Finally, Michael put down his bottle and leaned on the kitchen island.

"Sorry, baby."

"Well," she told him, her tone softening. "You should be. Do you think I'd let anything happen to her?"

"No, of course not. I just...."

"What?"

"I just can't believe how lucky I was to find you. And when we had Maria, it was the most amazing miracle. I'm just scared to lose all of it, you know?" He squinted his eyes to prevent the tears that were welling in them from falling.

Nicole marvelled at how her strong, sensible, husband could ever be vulnerable, but it was also partly why she loved him so much. A strong man is only sexy if he's not afraid to admit he can be hurt. It means that he has something more than just brain, or brawn. It means he has heart. A shell, regardless of its beauty, is undesirable unless you can hear the ocean in it; its sound is like a beautiful song and a heart is what gives a song its lyrics.

"Come on," she told him, taking his good hand, and leaving her drink on the island. "Come finish the tree with me."

Back in the living room, Michael pulled Maria from her chair and squeezed her plump little body against his hard one. Her eyes were hazel with specks of gold, like her mother, and like her mother, they were soulful.

"When's bedtime?"

"Is sex all you ever think about?"

Michael stared down his wife. "Really?"

"I thought it was funny. In about an hour. She needs her formula first."

Michael picked up the stuffed Santa Claus with the painted eyes and put the toy between him and Maria. Her giggles were contagious, and he laughed along with her.

"Come sei bella," he whispered, digging his nose into her chest. "Come tua madre."

"What are you two discussing over there?" Nicole was covered in tinsel, and she gave up trying to get it out of her cashmere sweater.

He put Maria back in her highchair and picked up his beer bottle from the coffee table. "I told her she's beautiful, like her mother."

"You charmer, you."

"You didn't think I was such a charmer when we first met."

"No. You're right. I thought you were a stalker."

"Again, really?"

"Yeah, really!"

"You're being awfully bad tonight, baby."

The heat between her legs was instant. She desired him. Since the day he saved her soul, she has given all of herself to him. She often stopped her mind from drifting to thoughts of the psychopath who mapped out their destiny for them, but she would never forget that it was Michael who gave his heart to her first. In following her to *Hayden's Park* that fateful day, he proclaimed his love for her.

She walked over to where he stood, took the bottle from his hand, and placed it back on the table. She grasped her sweater and pulled it over her head and dropped it to the floor. Her hands worked on unbuckling Michael's belt as he pulled her close to him and ran his hands up and down her back. Her lips met his just as words tried to pass them, "The baby…"

She undid the button of his jeans next, and then his zipper, and then she took his hands and placed them over the button of her own jeans, signaling him to take her.

"The baby will see that her parents are in love," she replied, pushing him so that he fell backwards on the couch.

"But…"

"But nothing…do you want me, or not?" she asked, irritated, and looking down at him as she straddled him with her hands on her hips.

Picking her up effortlessly, he tossed her on the empty couch cushion beside them. He hovered over her, supporting himself with his strong arms where every muscle was clearly defined. "What do you think?" he asked her, his long silky hair falling over his eyes.

She removed the hair from them and in his eyes, she saw a raw hunger so deep, she thought she would fall into the depths of his pupils

"I think," she replied, swallowing hard. "I'm in serious trouble."

"Finally. A right answer."

~

They were snuggled underneath a blanket. The baby monitor sat on the coffee table in front of them. It was the trophy of their lives. Maria slept soundly upstairs. She was a sleeper, like her father who always slept through the night. Nicole had teased him once by telling him that with all the espresso in his system, it was a miracle that he could sleep at all and that he must be a reverse vampire. She spent a week trying fruitlessly to cover up the hickey he gave her, pretending to "suck her blood" in rebuttal.

"I swear that I must be the only mother who has to check on the baby just to make sure she's breathing! That kid is too quiet," she whispered to him.

"You're an amazing mother, baby. I'm so proud of you," he whispered back, squeezing her hand.

"Do you want another one?"

"No. I'm pretty tired."

"Not beer, silly. Do you want another baby?"

Michael had thought about it. He did want another baby, a boy, so that they could round out their family. He envisioned himself handing over the keys to *Michael's Place*, just as his father had done with him.

"Yeah. I do."

Nicole turned her head to look him dead in the eyes. "You do?"

"Don't you?"

"Yeah, I really think I do. When do we start?" she asked, teasing him by running her hand over his chest.

He took her hand and held it against his heart. "Maybe tomorrow. Let's go to bed."

Nicole sat back on the couch and focused her attention on the television. "Just a few more minutes, honey. I want to hear the weather report. Kim invited me and Maria over for a play date tomorrow and I want to make sure we're not expecting freezing rain again."

"Okay."

Kim, a colourful, loud woman in her thirties with the vocabulary of a mobster, is Jacob's wife. Nicole liked her the minute they met. Kim and Jacob have two boys who sport the same blond hair as their parents. Kim asked Nicole and Maria if they wanted to help bake Christmas cookies in the morning, calling on Nicole's talents as a baker, and Nicole's old boss, Cathy had told her that whenever she was ready to go back to work, she always had a job at *Cathy's Confectioneries*.

Michael yawned, reminding Nicole of a lion, but it was a silent roar.

The familiar 11 O'clock News logo filled their television screen and Nicole strained to listen since the volume was down low – for the baby, Michael had said.

"Good evening, I'm Andrew Huntington and this is News Ottawa at 11. *We have breaking news at the top of the hour. Police have discovered a body in a single-family home in South Ottawa. The victim, a woman in her forties, was found by a family member after several failed attempts to reach the woman by telephone..."*

Michael was still holding Nicole's hand and he squeezed it harder.

"...Police say that the victim may have been deceased for at least twenty-four hours before being discovered. They described the woman as having several lacerations on her throat and that the woman was missing one eye, reminiscent of the Stevie Phelps murders."

"Christ..." Michael swore, leaning over to focus harder on the Newscasters words. Nicole had taken her hand back and both hands now covered her mouth.

"If anyone has any information regarding this case, they are asked to contact Ottawa Police at the number at the bottom of your screen. I am hesitant to call this a copy-cat murder, however, I urge

you to keep your doors and windows locked at all times. In other news..."

Michael stood abruptly and cursed as the blanket twisted around him. Marching over to the television, he turned it off by pounding his fist on the button. He stood with both hands on the television, his back to Nicole and his head bowed. Finally, he turned slowly to see his wife with her knees up, and her arms crossed over her chest. The look in her eyes suggested a mix of rage and anguish.

Michael saw himself as he stood on the carousel, a crowbar in his hands. He saw Nicole on the platform behind him, wearing the same look on her face as she was wearing now. Stevie's merciless laugh reverberated in his ears as if he was in the room with them. The echo had haunted Michael for weeks afterwards. He saw himself striking Stevie over, and over, the blood pouring from Stevie's forehead. The memory was a mixed cocktail of the macabre entangled with reality: a horror novel come to life.

Michael sat beside his wife and spoke carefully, a gentle tone perfuming his words, "It will be okay. You know that, right?"

"Will it? Will it, Michael? Didn't you hear what that news guy said? A copy-cat murder... there could be more!"

"Look, baby," he said, threading his fingers through his hair. "We don't know that yet. Okay? Just in case, though, I want you to stay home, tomorrow."

Nicole shook her head and sputtered the obvious. "Give me a break, Michael. Do you think staying home will save me? That poor woman died in her own *home*."

Again, Michael threaded his fingers through his hair. It was a nervous habit and standing, he paced the length of the carpet, stopping at the mantel. He was facing it when he said, "I don't believe this."

"Which part!?" Nicole called from the couch, forgetting

to keep her voice down. She pulled the blanket from her legs and joined him at the hearth. "What don't you believe? That the nightmare has begun again? That someone out there is mimicking Stevie? That I might lose my *damn* mind?"

Michael grasped her firmly by the shoulders and faced her, "No! I won't let that happen. *Not again...*" The last part was barely audible as his voice faltered.

"I'm scared," she said, pulling from his grasp. She looked just like she did the first time he had ever seen her at Vanessa Addison's grave who had been one of Stevie's victims. His wife was a woman in a child's nightmare.

"Come here," he told her, pulling her in again and trying to soothe her with kisses in her hair. Her body relaxed into him as she sobbed quietly into in his chest.

"We'll be okay," he whispered, feeling just like a liar.

He released her and held her with one arm around her waist, afraid to let go. Leading her to the stairwell, they ascended the stairs to their bedroom. It was a farce, he knew. He knew that this time, sleep would stay at bay.

Seven

Eric Summers sat at his desk at *The Herald,* chain smoking, and trying to make sense of the notes he was supposed to transcribe into a story. The new recruit's handwriting was illegible, and Eric scanned the room, looking for Jason Bryant, to interrogate him for details but the guy was no where to be seen.

Frustrated, Summers picked up his empty coffee cup and went to the office kitchen for a refill. His eyes ran over the back of Sandra's red jeans where they fit as if painted on. They had gone on one date, but Sandra ignored him after that. She had told her girlfriends that Eric was a leech and a cheap one, at that. He had made her pay for her own burger and fries, and it wasn't even a classy restaurant, unless he deemed *McDonalds* classy. She was the food editor for the paper, which made her disastrous dinner date with Summers that much funnier.

She noticed him, finally, and nodded. "Eric."

"Hi, Sandra."

She turned back to her conversation. She was talking with Colette in accounting, a sweet woman in her fifties who was notorious for leaving baked goods in the kitchen with notes attached: *Take one and Enjoy. (I said, one!)*, she always added, good-naturedly.

Eric pretended not to listen as the ladies resumed their conversation. His back to them, he slid a small silver flask from the inside pocket of his sport coat, held it in front of him and quickly poured whisky into his coffee. His secret vice was better than Jeff's not-so-secret Quaalude addiction, he reasoned.

"I heard, too," Colette was saying, pulling at her earlobe, nervously. "Do you think it's true?"

Sandra was enjoying one of Colette's double chocolate brownies and replied in between bites, "That it's a copy-cat killer? Could be. There are a lot of sickos out there these days."

Eric's ears perked but he didn't turn around.

"I hope not. I worry about the grandkids."

Sandra nodded, "How old are they now?"

"Tim is five, Mark is six, and little Adriana is three. Who's on the story?"

"Not sure yet. Jay is supposed to call a meeting, though."

Finally, Summers turned and walked over to the two women, sipping at his secret vice.

"A meeting?"

"Hi Eric, I haven't seen you in a while," Colette told him.

"Been working. You're looking good, Colette." She merely slapped at his arm in response. "What's this meeting?"

Sandra stood a good foot taller than Eric and the difference in height was almost a metaphor for the difference in their personalities. In both cases, she towered over him. "About the murder victim they found yesterday. The poor woman's eye was gouged out."

Colette cringed, and Summers spat a mouthful of coffee back into his cup. "Their eye? Like…Phelps?"

"The one and only… I have to get back to work. See you at the meeting."

Summers watched Sandra walk away and then turned to Colette who was offering him a brownie.

"No thanks. When's the meeting?"

"I'm not sure. Accounting's not part of those things. Maybe you should ask Jay. Are you sure you don't want a brownie? I made them fresh last night."

"Uh…sure," Eric said, plucking the biggest brownie off the tray. She placed it back on the kitchen table and turned to leave. It was nearing the end of her shift and she was Christmas shopping tonight with her husband, Robert, who vowed to get the shopping done early this year. It was a good thing that she had little patience for shopping malls. She scurried in and out of stores like a mouse on a mission with her husband behind her trying to keep up.

"See you, Eric," she said, eyeing her tray of brownies, as if quietly telling him to leave the rest for others.

"Yeah, see you."

Eric walked back to his desk, picked up his phone and dialed Jay's extension. Jay, a thirty-something Irishman with bright red hair, was the youngest Senior Editor at *The Herald* and he was always in his office, as if he was paying rent for the tiny square footage. Some staff called it his second home. He always answered the phone the same way, too. "Yeah."

"Hey, Jay. It's Eric."

"Yeah, Eric."

"When's the meeting? I heard Sandra talking about it just now."

"Tomorrow at nine, sharp. Anything else?"

Eric debated keeping his mouth shut but he asked him anyway, "I...why haven't I heard about it until now?"

"Didn't you get the memo?"

"No."

"Well, check your desk. Anything else?"

Jay was either deep into a story or interviewing someone for a story. Or, Eric thought to himself, just rude as hell by nature.

"No, that's it."

"See you tomorrow."

Eric hung up, placed a pencil between his teeth, and put his feet on the desk. If there was someone out there mimicking Stevie Phelps, it would be the most exciting development to date. It was also Eric's chance at another big break. He needed to write that story. He would bribe Jay with Irish Whiskey if he had to. He could already envision the byline.

"Copy-Cat Killer Mimics the Carousel Killer"
By Eric (in-your-face) Summers

There was no question about it now. He had to get the rights to writing the story, and maybe he could publish excerpts from it in his new book. He also needed pictures, and as he took the last swig of his coffee, he saw her face at the bottom of the cup. She was a hero, and a legend, and she was Stevie's killer. She was also married to a hot-tempered, six-foot Italian whose body was chiselled like one of those statues in Italy. Eric needed more than just spiked coffee. He needed a Quaalude.

Eight

Psycho Killer
Qu'est-ce que c'est
Fa-fa-fa-fa-fa-fa-fa-fa-fa-far better
Run run run run run run run away oh oh…

Michael stormed over to the ghetto blaster where it sat in the kitchen of his restaurant and turned the machine off almost knocking it off the shelf.

"Who the hell is playing this garbage!?" he growled.

"Geez, calm down, Mike. It's just a song."

Mo was in the kitchen surprised at his friend's reaction to *The Talking Heads.*

"Well, I don't want to hear it! Got it?"

"Yeah, we got it," Mo told him through clenched teeth.

Michael picked up the order for his table and left without another word.

"What the hell is wrong with *him?*" Mario asked Mo. "Don't know, but I'll try to find out."

"Good luck with that," Mario said, sarcastically. He turned his attention back to the eggplant he was frying for the Eggplant Parmesan on tonight's dinner menu, wishing the day would end.

Mo made his way to the dining room and found Michael sitting at the bar, a rock glass in front of him. It was just past noon and almost every table in the place was occupied, including one table with patrons that came straight from Parliament Hill.

Jacob was serving draft to a customer who was enjoying

a solo lunch. He was a man in a suit and tie, jotting notes on a yellow legal pad, wearing a Walkman.

Walking behind the bar, Mo picked up Michael's glass. "Refill?"

"Yeah."

"What is it?"

"Sambuca. Make it a double."

Mo eyed him, but he knew better than to say anything. Mike had that same look in his eyes he did the day that he asked for Mo's car keys to be able to drive to *Hayden's Amusement Park*. Mo didn't hesitate in handing over his keys. When a man like Michael Rossi needed something, he received it, no questions asked.

"Cover me. I need to change the keg."

"Need help, Jacob?"

"Nah. These arms are stronger than they look," he joked, flexing like Popeye.

Alone, Mo decided to try and get Michael to talk. "Rough day?"

He didn't answer and simply drank from the new Sambuca on ice that Mo had placed in front of him.

"What's with the mood?"

Finally, Michael stared at his friend and unleashed undeserving energy upon him. "What's it to you?"

"I'm your friend, Mike."

"Yeah, well, I just want to sit here, okay?"

"Suit yourself."

Mo began to walk away to replace empty peanut bowls that dotted the length of the bar, but he stopped and walked back over to his boss. "Whenever you're ready, you can talk to me."

Michael stared off into space, expressing his desire to be alone. Defeated, Mo walked away.

Michael was seething. This morning, he had leaned over and tried to greet Nicole with a good morning kiss, but she rolled away from him and got out of bed, telling him that she needed to check on the baby. After his shower and espresso, he tried to kiss her good-bye, and again, he received the cold shoulder. Thoughts of the recent murder had kept him awake all night and as much as he tried to rub at them, Stevie Phelps was before his eyes. The guy was dead. He was gone and yet, he still haunted Mike, swarming his brain like an ever-present headline before his eyes – *Carousel Killer, Carousel Killer, Carousel Killer.*

Nicole was already pulling away from him. He listened as she whimpered in her sleep, and he prayed that she wasn't reliving the rape in her dreams. The idea disgusted him. In a moment of weakness, she confided in him a few weeks after Stevie was killed that there had been a point when she thought that death would have been better. Remembering the rape was a fate worse than death. He had thrown the glass he was holding, clear across the room, aiming it towards an invisible Phelps. He held her into the night, rocking her like a child. The pain she carried inside of her, hurt him, as much as it hurt her. Slowly, she started to feel safe, and loved, and she emerged one day as the old Nicole – the fun, sexy, fearless woman who would bear his child.

"Mr. Rossi, a man at table eight wants to talk to you."

Michael turned to see one of his waitresses, Sylvia, standing next to him. She was a shy, young, girl with eyeglasses who could carry a tray of five dinners over her head.

"What's he want?"

"I… think he's upset, sir."

"About what?"

"The food."

"Thanks, Sylvia. I'll be right there."

Michael sighed. He didn't receive complaints about the food very often but when he did, he considered it a personal insult. He gazed toward table eight where two men were sitting. Both looked to be in their sixties. Downing the rest of his drink, Mike walked over to them.

"I'm the owner here. What seems to be the problem?"

One of the men wore a patch over his eye, while his friend

smoked a cigar. The man with the patch did the talking.

"I assume you're Michael?"

"Good guess. What's the problem?'

"The problem is that I ordered the Veal Cutlet and *Patate Fritte*, and it was a sloppy mess."

Michael looked down at the man's plate which was void of food. "But you ate it anyway?"

"Had to. I don't have time to order something else."

"What was so messy about it?"

The man smoking the cigar drank from his wine glass. His plate was wiped clean.

"The cutlet was overcooked, and the fries were cold."

"Are you some sort of cutlet expert?"

The man with the cigar smirked.

"What?"

"What makes you think it was overcooked?"

"Is this how you treat your customers?"

"It's a simple question."

The one-eyed man picked up his knife. "See this?" he asked, raising it towards Michael and twirling it between his fingers. "It wouldn't cut through the damn thing."

"I see. Thanks for the explanation. Lunch is on me."

Michael started to walk away but the man stopped him.

"Michael."

"What?" he asked, turning.

"Are you Italian?"

"What do you think?"

"Well," he said, taking the napkin from his lap and throwing it on his plate. "So am I. Let me know if you need any lessons."

"Lessons?"

"Yeah. Cooking."

Michael's blood boiled but he kept his cool, aware that several other diners were listening to the exchange. Clearing his throat, he told the man, "Lunch is on me and one dinner, too. Ask for me next time you come back."

Satisfied, the man grinned and nodded.

"*Asshole,*" Michael mumbled, walking away.

In his office, he sat behind his desk and lit a smoke. He picked up the phone and dialed. On the third ring, Nicole answered.

"Hey, baby."

"Hi."

"I thought you were going to Kim's house?"

"We are. As soon as Maria wakes from her nap."

"I miss you."

"I miss you too."

He expected more from her, but all he was greeted with was dead air. His smoke was gone in four long puffs.

"When will you be home?"

"I don't know. Aren't you stuck at the restaurant tonight, anyway?"

"Yeah, but…"

"But? Are you going to start with me again, Michael?"

"What the hell are you talking about?"

Nicole raised her voice, not caring about the consequences, "You don't care when I might be home, you're just trying to control me."

"Nic…"

"Admit it! Never mind, you don't have to admit it. I already know the truth but nothing, and I mean *nothing* you can do will guarantee my safety, Michael. I'm a big girl. I'll take care of myself. Talk to you later."

"I love you…"

She had hung up. His words hung on the air before him. Speaking to himself, they signified nothing.

"*Dammit!!*"

He pushed the phone across the desk so that it fell to the floor with a crash. He got up from his chair and swung his office door open, marched over to the bar, and walked around it. Both Jacob and Mo stared as he took the entire Sambuca bottle, along with a glass, back to his office. He slammed the door shut: A *Do Not Disturb* without words.

"Shit."

"Yeah. Something's wrong with him."

"He won't tell you what it is?"

"You know Mike."

Jacob did know Mike and Mo was right. Something was wrong with him. It was the first time since he's known him that Michael completely neglected his tables. Mike was proud of the restaurant and of his work. One time, he had fired a new hire on the spot for disrespecting an elderly couple by ignoring the old man, every time he raised one hand in need.

He's seen Michael drunk before too, and he hoped that he wasn't about to polish off an entire bottle of booze. Then there would really be something to worry about, and the only person who could pull him out of it was baking cookies with his wife. He almost wanted to call Kim and warn her, but if Michael found out, there wouldn't be enough places for Jacob to hide. When Michael saw red, it became the only colour in the spectrum.

Nine

"Has he come out yet?"

"No."

Three hours later, Michael had still not come out of his office.

"Maybe we should check on him," Jacob said.

"Are you nuts?" Mo was filling the garnish station, prepping for dinner service.

"I'll call him then. Pretend I need something."

Jacob walked over to the phone that sat beside the cash register and held his breath as he dialed Mike's extension.

"What?"

"Hey, Mike. What…uh, signature cocktail do you want to pair with the specials tonight?"

"I don't care," Mike told him, slurring his words. "Make something up."

The dial tone that followed filled Jacob's ears.

"Well?" Mo asked.

"He's bad off."

"Wonderful."

A man wearing a fedora approached them. Eric Summers had tried calling the Rossi household, but no one was home. He debated with himself, but he had little time to waste and decided to seek Nicole out at the restaurant. If her husband was around, he'd simply leave, he reasoned. He was used to taking chances. The last chance he took won him national recognition. Although he wasn't keen on getting his arm broken at the hand of a hot-blooded Italian, it was a free country and he feigned needing a drink when he sat himself at the bar which wasn't far from the truth considering the meeting this morning.

Jay had informed everyone that he would be writing the story on the recent copy-cat murder and if anyone had any new leads, to let him know immediately. No amount of Irish Whiskey would change Jay's mind and considering that Summers wanted to keep his job, he kept his mouth shut and decided to focus on his book instead.

Mo placed a coaster in front of Summers and a fresh bowl of peanuts.

"What'll it be?"

"A beer. Draft."

"Coming right up."

Mo walked over to pour a draft and the man addressed Jacob, "Is Nicole Rossi around?"

"No, she's not. Does she know you're here?"

"Yeah," Eric lied. "I guess she forgot to meet me."

"Sorry," Jacob told him.

Eric picked at the peanuts, dropping the shells on the bar causing Jacob to place an empty bowl in front of him.

"Thanks."

The door to the office opened. Michael stood wobbling in the threshold, straightened his back, and stumbled over to the bar. The minute he could focus his eyes, he recognized the fedora.

"What in the *hell* are you doing here?"

Summers didn't answer him and shucked another peanut.

"He was supposed to meet Nicole," Jacob offered.

Eric popped the peanut in his mouth and stood, ready to make his escape. "I don't want any trouble, Rossi. I was just leaving."

Michael stepped to the side, trapping Eric against the bar. "You're here to see my wife?"

"I…was hoping to see her, yeah…" Eric stammered, smelling the alcohol on Mike's breath as it wafted towards him.

"What did I tell you at the diner?"

Jacob listened, trying to decode the conversation. It dawned on him that this was the guy who pretended to be interested in writing a story about *Michael's Place*. He knew Mike was meeting him at *Kay's Diner*.

"Look," Eric said, trying to sound tough. "I know you're not interested, but maybe she is."

A smile curled on Michael's lips, and it wasn't put there by merriment.

"That's what you think, eh?"

"Uh…yeah. She can think for herself, can't she?" Michael leaned forward menacingly.

"Get away from me, you *freak*."

"What did you call me?"

"Did your ears burn off too?"

Summers didn't know where he was gathering his courage from, but if he was about to get the life beat out of him, he had nothing to lose.

"Mike…" Jacob said trying to diffuse the situation. "Let him go."

"Shut up, kid!" Mike told him. Turning back to Eric, he enunciated his words ever-so-slowly. "Be like the *Goddamn* snake you are and slither back into your hole. My wife is off limits to you. Understand?"

Eric's back was arched as he fruitlessly tried to put space between him and the man who looked like he'd enjoy strangling him, and the only weapon Eric had access to was the pencil behind his ear.

Mo had returned and watched silently until he was forced to intervene. There were still a few customers in the restaurant, and he knew that no matter how drunk Mike was, he wouldn't want to do anything that might jeopardize his reputation.

Mo walked around the bar and placed one hand on Michael's arm. "He's not worth it, Mike."

Instinctively, Michael raised his fist and clocked Mo in the mouth with the back of his hand.

"Jesus Christ…" Jacob mumbled as he also made his way

around the bar.

"Mo, I'm sorry...I..."

While Michael's attention was focused on his friend, Summers inched past and walked swiftly to the front door, letting himself out.

"Are you happy now, Mike?" Mo asked him, touching his lip where it was bleeding.

Jacob stood between them, unsure of what to say.

"Are you happy?" Mo repeated. "Why don't you go the hell home and sleep it off?"

Instead of relenting, the opposite took place. "Home? *Home?* There's nothing for me at home."

"Don't be crazy, buddy, of course there is," Jacob offered.

"What do you know, kid!? Leave me *alone*, the both of you. Sorry about your lip, Mo. Send me a bill."

They watched as Michael went back to his office and emerged a moment later wearing his coat. Jacob rushed to the front door ahead of him.

"Are you driving?"

"Get out of my way."

"Are you driving?"

"No! Okay? I'm walking. Now get out of my way, kid. I mean it."

Jacob opened the door and let his boss out. He looked after him, watching as Michael made his way down the sidewalk instead of the parking lot behind the building. When he was satisfied that he was telling the truth, Jacob went back to the bar and picked up the phone.

"Hey, honey. Let me speak with Nic."

"Why? Her hands are covered in cookie dough!"

"Let me speak with her, *now*."

"Okay, but this better be good, mister."

Nicole was on the line in seconds.

Ten

At *Oak Park Cemetery,* Michael stood freezing, his hands stuffed into the pockets of his jeans. His knuckles hurt from where they met Mo's teeth. Dark clouds blanketed the sun and there was a dampness in the air that he could almost touch. He shivered from a place deep inside. The cold had nothing to do with it.

A young couple stood at a grave site close to him. They had one arm across the other's shoulder. They were huddled together for warmth, he thought. Later he would realize that they were holding on to each other to keep from falling down – in grief.

Michael looked before him at the marker engraved with both of his parents' names. Even in death, they wanted to be close to each other. A flashback of his parents crossed his eyes. They were all three sitting at the dinner table. His mother was serving them soup and when Michael looked down at his bowl, he saw nothing but a few pieces of bread floating around in a clear broth. He looked up at his father who had stuck a napkin in his shirt collar and dug in ravenously, quickly finishing one bowl and asking for another. Michael had taken a sip, and the broth was light and almost tasteless. The bread was toasted from butt ends of loaves gone dry. They were sautéed in butter and only a few leaves of parsley floated around the bowl as if to decorate it. It was a bad week. There was nothing else to eat, but his father made it seem like it was a meal fit for a King allowing Michael's mother to sleep better at night. The memory brought a lump to Michael's throat. Despite the hardships they faced, his parents' love for each other never wavered.

He thought of Nicole and his anger returned. Only hours earlier, they were home, making love, oblivious to the news of the recent murder. In hours, everything seemed to change, and he was angry with her for betraying his trust. In pulling away from him, she betrayed her wedding vows: *Through bad times and in good.* He looked at his hand and his wedding ring. In his mind's eye, the circle was cracked.

He was clearly remembering the day she placed the ring on his finger.

The Priest that had married them was the same one who had baptized Michael. He lived adjacent to the Church and Nicole was waiting in a room, in his rectory, when she heard someone knocking softly at her door. She had placed her hands on the door and with the side of her face against it, she whispered, "Who is it?"

"It's me."

"Michael? What are you doing out there?"

"I miss you."

"We're about to be married."

"I know, baby. I can't wait, you know."

His own face was against the door and with only the wood between them, he admitted, "I want to make mad, passionate, love to you, baby."

Giggling, she replied, "That's scandalous! Now, go away before Father Carmine finds you!"

"Okay, I'm going now."

A minute passed. She was still at the door and whispered to the wood, "Are you still there?"

Silence greeted her, and just as she was about to walk away, she heard a faint, "Yeah."

After the ceremony, she told him, "My life begins today."

That night, in a grove just outside of town, they turned a camping tent into a make-shift Bridal Suite. Crickets sang a symphony. Michael watched his new bride as she undressed, a blush to her cheeks. She crawled into bed which he constructed from only a flat mattress and a lonely sheet. There was an ever-present heat between them and it mingled with the humidity of the summer night.

"I realized something today, Michael."
"That you're a wife now?" he teased.
"That my name sounds better next to yours."
"You're so beautiful, Nic."
She threw a smile at him, and he captured it underneath his fingertips vowing to give it back to her whenever she needed it.

Michael kissed his hand and laid it on top of the headstone. He pulled a smoke from the package in his coat pocket, lit it, and walked away. The young couple had left. He stopped in the same spot where they had been standing. The name on the headstone read, *Shawna Lorraine Costner, 1982-1982*. A baby. A new lump arose in Mike's throat. He longed to hold Maria. He needed her like he needed his next breath. Quickly, he made his way through the park and out the wrought iron archway that marked the exit, his baby before his eyes, her mother behind her.

~

At home, he opened the front door to find Nicole sitting on their couch. One hand still on the doorknob, he looked at her for a few seconds and then shut the door and took off his coat. Staring at the hall tree, his hands hanging on to his coat that he placed over one hook, he asked her, "Still mad at me?"

"I'm not mad, Michael."

He released his coat and turned to her. "Where's the baby?"

"At Kim's. She offered to keep her overnight."

"What? Why would she do that?" His arms already felt empty.

"Are you still drunk, Michael?"

The light of understanding registered in his eyes. "I'm going to kill that kid."

"No, you're not," Nicole said, rising from her seat. "What's gotten into you?" she asked him, standing before him.

"Into *me*? What about *you*?"

"What about me?"

He reached out to take her in his arms, and she stepped backwards. "*That!* Exactly *that!* Why can't I touch you?"

Nicole held herself around her waist and walked back to the couch. Michael stormed over to where she was sitting and sat next to her, careful to leave a space between them.

"Talk to me, baby. *Please*."

"They found another body," she told him, emotionless.

"Where? When?"

"At the river. This morning before sunrise. I heard it on the car radio when I was coming home."

Michael's hands met his hair. He asked, afraid, "Were the eyes...?"

"Cut out," Nicole reported, still holding herself around the waist.

"Jesus..." he stared at his lap for a minute and then met her eyes. "You're remembering, aren't you? You're remembering, and you don't want me to touch you because...."

"*Don't*," she said, gritting her teeth.

"Don't what?"

"Don't make me feel guilty for something that I can't control!"

"I'm not!"

"Yes. You are." She was looking at him as if he was a stranger and Michael felt the gap widen so that the small space between them felt as long as the Nile. Rising from the couch, she headed towards the stairwell.

"Where are you going?"

"To take a bath."

"We aren't done here yet, Nic."

Her hand on the banister, one foot on the first stair, she stated flatly, "Yes. We are. Please don't come to bed drunk. Good night."

"Good night? It's 4:30!"

She pretended not to hear him. She quickly made her way to the bathroom, shut the door, and turned on the bathtub faucet. Only then did she allow herself to cry; a muffled cry underneath the noise of the water running. When she was finished with her bath, she went back downstairs to make herself toast and was met with an empty house. Michael was gone.

Eleven

Downtown, at the precinct, Detective Valetti sat at his desk, an open file folder in front of him. A bottle of Scotch occupied the bottom drawer and he thought to take a swig, to ease his trembling hands. He pulled off his eyeglasses and rubbed at the bridge of his nose. Putting them back on, he resumed reading.

The victim was stripped of her jeans and underwear which were found discarded nearby. Blood ran the length of her navel to mid-thigh. Tests have determined that it is her own blood, O-Positive. Further tests have determined that the woman was approximately six weeks pregnant.

"I hate my job," Valetti said out loud.

Lacerations were found in the woman's groin. Consistent with the murder of Roxanne Halpenny, the victim's left eye was removed with a sharp object, most likely a blade from a knife.

He scanned the rest of the report and felt his insides lurch.

"Becky, get in here!" Valetti didn't bother to use his office phone and called for his assistant by raising his voice.

"Yes, sir?"

"What's the meaning of this?"

"What do you mean?"

"The report is unfinished."

"No sir, I typed it the way it was given to me."

"Are you sure?"

Becky, a woman in her forties, grew impatient. "Of course, I'm sure."

"Where is the evidence list?"

"There was no evidence, Sam."

She's worked for Valetti for nearly twenty years, and somewhere along the line, she stopped calling him Detective Valetti. Their relationship was more that of husband and wife, minus the love.

Valetti stared at the file. Normally, there would be something left at the scene of the crime, even if it was just half a *Goddamn* fingerprint.

"Carry on," he told his assistant who swore a little under her breath and went back to her desk.

Puzzled, he picked up his phone and called Ray. "Detective Lalonde."

"Ray, it's me."

"Hungry again?"

Ray laughed at his friend who caused the unnecessary scene at lunch time, today. Valetti had bet him twenty bucks that he could get a free lunch, even after devouring his first plate. Ray was out forty since he scored a free dinner too.

"Funny. What's going on with this case? No evidence with Halpenny and now Cutter, too?"

"I have forensics on it."

"And?"

"And nothing. They haven't found anything."

"How is that even possible? Not semen?"

"Nope."

"Hair?"

"Not a one."

Ray still had a cigar between his lips. "The killer knows what he's doing. I don't know… but when I learn more, you'll be the first man I call."

"Fine," Valetti told him, hanging up.

Picking up the phone once more, he dialed Ray again.

"Miss me?"

"I need a drink. Care to join me?"

"Damn straight I would, but the wife will kill me. We're having her sister over for dinner tonight. Speaking of which, I gotta run."

Valetti hung up a second time by pressing his fingers on the hook. He dialed home next.

"Hi, honey."

"Sam, when are you coming home?"

"Not for a while yet. I have a ton of things to work out here. Go ahead and eat without me."

"Again?"

"Sorry, honey. I love you."

Elise sighed. "I love you, too. Be safe."

Valetti stood from his office chair, groaning as his back cracked a little. He grabbed his coat and gloves and walked past Becky at her desk.

"I'm leaving."

"And a good night to you, too, Sam."

She watched as he left, a slight look of concern on her face. When he was working on a case, he was a different man. It was as if his life depended on solving it.

Twelve

Two Years Ago, December 24th, 1980

"We know this is very difficult for you, Miss Harte. Would you like some water?"

Nicole sat stoically, with her back straight, staring straight ahead. The only movement she made was with her nails as they scratched the table before her. The dimness in the room was in stark contrast to the bright lights in the main precinct where some officers were indulging in Eggnog and celebrating the day, anxious to get home. Criminals were oblivious to the day of the year, however, and most officers were stuck at the precinct, intent on treating themselves – for the sake of Jesus.

For forty minutes she answered the officers' questions, feeling like she did in her final year of college, when she was taking her exams. Just like then, her responses would help pave the road she would forever follow.

"Is he…dead?"

The two officers looked at each other curiously. Officer Black was the older of the two and he spoke with a tender tone.

"Is who dead, Miss Harte?"

He knew the woman's boyfriend was in the hospital being treated for burns. Stevie Phelps had managed to light Michael Rossi on fire, before suffering his own fate at the hands of the woman who sat before him.

"Stevie," Nicole answered without emotion.

"Yes, he is."

Officer Black glanced at his colleague who was leaning against the wall next to the door, his arms crossed. They shared a *look that asked without words, "Is she stable?"*

"That's why we're here," Officer Black continued. "You last mentioned that Phelps was pursuing you with the intent to harm. Do you affirm that statement?"

Nicole stared quietly at Officer Black and then twisted her head to seek answers in the eyes of his colleague, but only she held the answers, and the officers' job was to try and extract them.

Officer Goldsmith was a young man with blond hair who reminded her of Jacob. His jaw moved up and down, making it obvious that he was chewing gum, and Nicole imagined herself slapping his face to make him stop.

She wanted desperately to see Michael. Moments after she impaled Stevie on the horn of the plastic carousel unicorn, she could hear the unmistakable sound of police sirens drawing near. Michael had called 9-1-1 before setting out to find her at Hayden's Park. *In police terminology, he called them as back-up.*

Four cruisers pulled up outside the park that day and as uniformed men and women made their way towards her, Nicole didn't feel comforted. She felt like she was the one who was about to face condemnation.

Officer Goldsmith was losing his patience. His wife was at home eating Christmas Eve dinner with their friends and family, and he resented that fact since he was the one who prepped the Honey Ham. Not to mention he loathed leftovers.

"Miss Harte?" *He spoke to Nicole's back and this time, she didn't look at him.*

"Yes," *Nicole stammered.* "That's right. He said that I would pay for what I said. That I would pay for calling him a bastard."

"Did he have a weapon?" *Officer Black asked.*

"None that I could see at the time, no."

Black read from a report in his hands, "Stevie hit Michael over the head with a sledgehammer. *Do you recall these words as you spoke them at the crime scene when making your statement?"*

"Yes, I do."

"But Phelps didn't pursue you with the hammer?"

"No, he dropped it in the snow, as soon as…"

"Take your time, Miss Harte."

"As soon as he hit Michael..."

"Did you witness his attack on Mr. Michael Rossi?" Imagining Stevie attacking the man she loved, Nicole lost control of her emotions. She shifted and sat on her hands, letting her tears ride down on her cheeks.

"Yes."

"Can you explain in detail, what happened?"

"John, she already made a full statement."

Officer Black looked at Goldsmith and nodded. He was a thorough man, and this wasn't a simple shop-lifting case. It was murder, and when he would write up the paperwork, he wanted to be absolutely sure that he could add, "in self-defence", releasing her from any criminal wrongdoing. He turned to Nicole again, "You asserted that Stevie Phelps raped you in October of this year. Do you maintain that assertion?"

Her face contorted and between gasps for air, she told them, "I'll...take that water, now."

"Get her some water, Chris."

Officer Goldsmith left the room and Black waited. There was a reason that two men were to be present with the witness at all times, and that was so that any statement made could be processed by two minds, and two sets of ears.

Goldsmith returned with a coffee cup full of water and handed it to Nicole who gulped it down eagerly. She wiped a few drops from her chin with the back of her sleeve and then placed the cup down in front of her. A package of cigarettes sat on the table before her, and she eyed it. She had quit smoking but craved one now like a dying man craves another minute of life.

"I maintain that assertion, yes."

Satisfied, Goldsmith looked at his watch and wondered if he could still make it home for dessert. His colleague, however, wasn't finished.

"Why didn't you report the rape when it happened, Miss Harte?"

"Ex...excuse me?"

"John…"

"We're here to determine whether you did indeed kill Stevie Phelps in self-defence, and I think your answer is determinate on this."

Nicole's demeanour suddenly changed. She could feel the sweat on the nape of her neck and no amount of water would extinguish the fire in her belly. She saw Michael before her, and she saw the look in his eyes when she first admitted to him that Stevie had raped her. The fury on his face registered immediately, and she could hear him whispering in her ear. Like a ventriloquist, he was doing the talking and she was his puppet.

"Am I on trial!? Am I being charged with something? Because if I am, I would like a lawyer. But I'm pretty certain, officer, that the world will not be mourning the loss of a man like Stevie Phelps. Had I not killed him, he would have tortured, raped, and killed someone else. Had I not killed him, he'd be out there right now, laughing at all of you while my body lay in the morgue, probably next to Michael's."

Goldsmith was now in front of Nicole, leaning on a chair with both hands, while Black assumed a position with his arms crossed, showcasing a mermaid tattoo. The two men looked at each other. Goldsmith was warning Black with his eyes, trying to tell him not to push the woman too far, or the captain would have his head.

Adopting an even gentler tone, Black prodded, "Can you please answer the question, though, Miss…"

"Because he violated me in the most non-sacred of ways and I was not eager to tell a stranger just exactly how! Okay? Would you want your wife, or sister, or daughter to go through that?" she asked him, talking with her hands, just like Michael would. "Would you want your loved one scrutinized like a common criminal? 'Oh, what did she do to deserve *that*,' people would wonder. Don't make me laugh, officer. I'm not really in the mood for a chuckle."

She paused, feeling her entire body tremble with nervous energy. She had killed someone, and the truth behind those words made her physically sick. The other part of her felt a release so powerful, she was almost happy. She was happy to know that no one else would need to suffer at the hands of the madman that some were *calling,* "The Carousel Killer".

Through clenched teeth, she asked Black, "Can I please go now? I need to get to the hospital."

Without waiting for Black to speak, Goldsmith told her, "Yes. We have your information, should we have further questions. You're free to leave, Miss Harte. You can ask the officer at the administration desk to call you a taxi if you need it."

Nicole scraped her chair across the floor and stood next to the door, waiting for one of the men to let her out. Goldsmith walked over to her and opened the door and then shut it again slightly.

"On behalf of the Ottawa Police and the citizens of this city, I want to personally thank you for what you did today."

"That's enough, Officer Goldsmith."

Chris ignored his colleague's reprimand. "I hope," *he continued, addressing Nicole,* "that you can find some peace on this Christmas Eve."

Stunned, Nicole's mouth gaped open slightly, but she simply nodded and stared at the door handle, once again seeking permission to leave. Goldsmith opened the door and asked an officer standing in the hallway outside to escort Nicole out, as she was free to go.

"What the hell do you think you're doing? You know you can't say the slightest thing that would deem you biased against the case."

"It's Christmas, John, and that girl acted in self-defence. You know it, and I know it. The whole damn precinct knows it!"

John Black spent his life playing by the rules but as he looked at his colleague, fifteen years his junior, he realized he was right. He also realized that Nicole Harte was right and Stevie Phelps' death, as sinful as it sounds, was a cause for celebration.

"Go home, John. Go eat your turkey or whatever it is you and Tracy eat."

Black wiped at his brow with a handkerchief he pulled from his sport coat pocket that was embroidered with his monogram. It had been a wedding gift from his wife.

"I'll hand it over to Valetti."

"The Harte investigation?"

"No. The Phelps murders."

Goldsmith nodded, "Good man."

He pulled on the door again, stopped, and added, "Merry Christmas."

"Merry Christmas."

Alone, Officer Black stared at the oak table in front of him. It was covered in markings where hundreds of suspects had nervously scratched their nails in the wood. Had he taken a closer look, he would have seen the beginning of the letter "M", made fresh only moments earlier by a woman who would soon go down in history. "M", for "Michael."

Thirteen

He tip-toed around his own house stealthily. If Elise woke to find that he was just coming home, he'd be up for another hour, listening to her endless tirade.

It was one in the morning, and he had spent the last few hours drinking Scotch at *Fox's Pub.* An old man sat next to him regaling him with stories from his time spent in Paris. Sam had never been to Paris. In fact, he has never been out of the country. He and Elise were married in Nova Scotia where she grew up as the youngest of five siblings. A lighthouse provided the backdrop for their nuptials, while friends and family looked on. Afterwards, they feasted on lobster, and danced on the beach, and when the sun went down, they lit the most marvellous bonfire. There was a tradition that Elise's family followed that entailed burning a childhood memento as a symbolic transition from little girl to wife. She made Sam grasp the other arm of her first doll and then they swung the toy as if it were a real girl and thrust it into the fire.

At the time, Sam had thought the tradition creepy, but afterwards, as Elise sat between Sam's legs, her white dress flowing around them in the sand, he felt nothing but love for his new bride and he held her against his chest where his heart beat with unconditional love.

They had met at a small grocery store. The kind where the aisles are only two feet wide and the canned goods are stacked haphazardly, and the dirty magazines are on full display next to *Country Home* and *Good Housekeeping.* Sam's best friend at the time, Martin, ran the store and when Sam was there to stock up on sugar and milk, he noticed the woman with the dark curls, and perfect mouth standing in the bakery aisle reading a box of shortening.

"Who's that?"

"She just moved to the neighbourhood. Got your eye on her, Sam?"

Sam looked at his friend as if to say, Who wouldn't? "Is she single?"

"Never seen her come in with anyone. Stick around till she's ready to check out. I'll look for a ring."

Sam stood next to the magazines, pretending to read Cars and Motorcycles, and waited impatiently. When Elise finally made her way to the register, he followed her hand like he was following a house fly in an attempt to kill it. Her finger was bare, and she left the store before he could get the gumption to say anything.

"She's here every Tuesday at exactly 10 a.m," Martin told him, reading his friend's mind.

Every Tuesday for the rest of the month, Sam found himself buying things he didn't need, like dental floss, rope, mulch, and one time, he even placed a bottle of women's shampoo in his cart.

"It's a lovely brand. I use the same one as your wife." Elise had spoken to him first. Confused, he looked down at his cart and realized his mistake.

"Oh, I'm not married."

"You're not?"

"No...I like to use that brand."

Her laughter filled the small store, startling even Martin "I am not that naïve. Just ask me."

"Ask you?"

"To dinner. That's why you're here, isn't it?"

Giving up the ruse, he told her, "Yes. Would you like to go to dinner with me?"

He stared at her perfect red mouth, willing the word to escape from it.

"Ask me again next Tuesday," she told him, walking away. Her perfume lingered around him for the rest of the day and two

Tuesdays later, she finally accepted his invitation to dinner.

He made his way up the stairs, hanging on to the banister for dear life. He was drunk. He had left the bar at midnight and although it was only five blocks from his house, it took him an hour to get home. He drove the back roads at a snail's pace, unwilling to take any chances. The last thing he needed was to get pulled over for hitting something, or someone.

He could see a faint light on at the end of the hallway. Elise always kept a night-light on for her husband and when he reached their bedroom, he was relieved to hear his wife snoring. She had trouble sleeping and relied on sleeping pills and he managed to elude the fight that would have ensued had she noticed the hour – and the alcohol on his breath.

He undressed quickly and slid underneath the covers and snuggled up next to his wife. She was a good actress. He thought she was asleep. Her back was to him. He didn't know that her eyes were wide open.

Fourteen

The headache started at the back of his head and circled his skull to reach his temples. The sunlight forced him to open his eyes and see the empty spot next to him. Michael picked up his wristwatch from the nightstand. It was past eleven in the morning and just about time for lunch at *Michael's Place*. Despite what happened yesterday, he knew that his staff would have his back, and take care of the restaurant for him. When he was recovering from his burns, Mo took over as manager, while Jacob worked full time at the bar, and Mario was in charge of the food operations. It was his ship, but his crew steered it like their own.

Yesterday, when Nicole had barricaded herself in the bathroom, he had set off aimlessly with his camera. He didn't want to leave her, but she had made it abundantly clear that she wasn't going to speak with him or cuddle with him like he desired her to do. He set off, walking downtown streets and alleyways, until the sun set, causing the air to grow frigid. A light snow fell, and Michael wore only his leather jacket. He sought warmth in a small, dingy pool hall, where he downed half a dozen beers that mixed precariously with the Sambuca that was already gurgling in his system. He played a few sloppy games of pool, giving up, eventually, and snapping shots of various objects on his table. He took a picture of his beer mug, half empty. In jest, he took a second shot and called it, "half full". A woman at a neighbouring table who wore loud, baby blue eyeshadow, and had her hair teased sky high, flirted with him by crossing and uncrossing her legs that were housed in a black, leather, micro-mini. Finally, Michael raised his hand to show her his wedding ring. *"What about it? Wrong hand, cowboy."* Michael had sneered at her, threw a twenty-dollar bill on the table, and left. By the time he arrived home, Nicole was already asleep.

He got out of bed and like a ton bricks, fell to the cold, hardwood floor, and began with ten push-ups. Every muscle in his body ached but he persisted, sucking in the taut muscles of his abdomen, counting out ten more, and then twenty more – feeling the sweat form all over his naked torso. Like a self-inflicted torture, he stopped counting at one hundred and fell to the ground, his head in his arms, breathing heavily. The night had taken its toll on him.

He got up and found a white t-shirt. Pulling it over his head, he left the bedroom, making note of the fact that the house was too quiet.

In the kitchen, next to the espresso maker, he found a note where Nicole had left it on a page in the middle of her notebook: *"Went to pick up Maria. Grounds are already in the maker, just heat it up. – N"*

Mike put the machine on the burner of the stove and waited until the gas came to life underneath. He walked back over to the book. Taking it in his hands, he flipped to the first few pages: *She likes applesauce with a sprinkle of sugar on top.* On a different page, he read: *Remember to look into Daycares.* He flipped back to where the built-in ribbon marked today's date: *Went to pick up Maria...* She hadn't even told him she loved him. He threw the book on the kitchen island to address the espresso maker that was screaming signaling that the coffee was ready. Pouring himself a cup, he added two espresso spoons full of sugar from the sugar bowl that sat next to the stove omitting his usual shot of Sambuca.

He drank from his cup, staring out the kitchen window for a while, following a mother pulling a red wagon behind her with his eyes. The little girl was dressed in a pink winter coat and love surged through his heart. His father once told him that he was his legacy, and not the pizzeria. At that moment, Michael fully understood what his pop was trying to say: A human heart has the ability to implode even brick and mortar.

Taking a package of cigarettes from the kitchen table, Michael pulled a smoke from it, lit it, and walked back over to the island. The page had changed when he threw the book down. It was turned one page over. The 4 o'clock slot was circled, and her unmistakable script filled the space next to it: *Meet Edward at Kay's Diner.*

Instantly, jealousy coursed through his veins. He walked back to the kitchen table where he kept his reading glasses. Putting them on, he tried to make sense of the entry as if the eyeglasses would magically interpret the words etched in blue ink. He had never once heard Nicole speak of a man named Edward. He slammed the book shut and dropped it as if it was about to bite him. With a smoke between his lips, he paced back and forth for a few minutes, trying to think. *Kay's Diner* was just down the street from their house. She was meeting the guy at four o'clock. Was she going to take Maria with her? Who was the guy?

He looked at the clock and it was a quarter to twelve. If she had gone to pick up Maria, they would be home soon. Michael took off his glasses and left them on the kitchen island next to the notebook. Thinking twice about it, he picked up the glasses and put them back on the kitchen table where he always sat to work on the day's crossword puzzle. He ran out of the room and up the stairs to get dressed. He didn't want to be there when Nicole got back. As much as he desperately wanted to kiss his daughter, he didn't want the baby to witness a fight. She would deny everything, he knew. She would lie to him, and she might even try to place blame on him. He wasn't going to let that happen. He had a different plan and as he thought about it now, a six-letter word for "dread", ran through his mind: *Edward.*

~

At *Michael's Place,* the dining room was packed. Curtis stood in the middle of the room at his makeshift workstation, flipping a pizza high in the air and catching it expertly with one hand, the dough still spinning beneath his fingers. Cheers erupted throughout the room amplifying Michael's headache.

At the bar, he asked Mo to follow him to his office while Jacob looked after them, curious. Michael closed his door and motioned for Mo to take a seat, staring guiltily at his friend's lip where it was bruised purple.

"Look, Mo," he stated, skipping the pleasantries. "I'm sorry."

Mo sat quietly, scrutinizing the dark shadows underneath Michael's eyes. Mo was not only Michael's friend, but he was also Maria's Godfather, and although he was still angry, he wasn't about to let a bruised lip kill years of friendship or ruin a life-long relationship with his Goddaughter.

He put out his hand to indicate he forgave Michael, and Michael took it and squeezed it.

Mike sat back in his leather chair and ran his fingers through his long, straight, black hair.

"So, are you going to talk to me, now?"

"It's Nic," Michael stated flatly, taking the smoke from behind his ear and lighting it.

"What's going on?"

"The news. The copy-cat killer. You've heard?"

Mo's wife had told him about the recent murders in the city. He felt stupid for not figuring it out on his own. His friends were reliving a horrific past – one that had almost changed the course of their lives, and that almost ended Michael's life.

"Yeah, Veronica told me. Then I read it in the paper. Jesus, Mike, I should have put two and two together. Is Nic okay?"

Michael stared at the picture on his desk of Nicole and Maria. His wife held the baby on her lap underneath a Willow tree. It was Autumn when he captured them through the lens of his camera, and he and Nicole both laughed when Nicole covered the baby up to her chest in leaves of various hues. Maria's giggles echoed throughout the empty park. The scene was idyllic, and it felt like years ago.

Still staring at the picture, he simply said, "No."

Michael stood and walked around the small space of his office. Mo followed him by swivelling in his chair. "What's going on?"

Sitting on the edge of his desk, Michael crushed out his smoke in an ashtray. "She's pulling away from me. She won't let me touch her," he admitted. "She's scared, and I don't know how to help her." Sitting back in his chair, he leaned over with both elbows on the desk, his fists clenched. "Then this morning, I found a note in her notebook. She's meeting some guy named Edward at four o'clock today. I have no idea who he is."

"You don't think she's…cheating on you?"

"I don't know. Maybe."

Mo shook his head back and forth, "No. No, Mike, she wouldn't do that. She loves you. You have a family now."

"Then *who* is he!?" Michael asked him, raising his voice.

Mo's wife called him Peter Parker. He always said he had a "Spidey Sense" about people and that he was usually right. In the short time he's known Nicole, she's never given him cause to doubt her, or her love for his friend. There had to be a different explanation, one that would appease Michael's hidden insecurities.

"Why don't you just ask her?"

"Because… " Mike said, lowering his voice and slouching with his hands deep in his pockets. "I'm afraid she'll lie to me."

Mo could see the dilemma his friend was suffering through. He was in love with the woman of his dreams, but she used to describe her past as something sordid and wicked, as if she had been responsible for causing the rape. If lying helped her retain her sanity, then it was possible that she would resort to telling untruths, even if it meant hurting her husband.

"What are you going to do, then?"

"Follow her," Michael stated, surprising his friend with his monotone.

"Wait. Are you sure about that? She might see you. Where is she going?"

"The diner by our house."

"*Kay's?* That place is tinier than this office. She'll see you, Mike."

"Well, what the hell am I going to do then?"

Mo pondered for a few seconds, staring at the wall beside him. "Rick," he said, speaking to the wall.

"Rick?"

"We'll send Rick," he repeated, looking at Mike. "She hasn't met him yet. She'll never know he's there to watch her."

"You want me to ask one of my employees to spy on my wife?"

"Do you have a better idea?"

Michael swivelled in his chair so that his back was to Mo. He stared at the painting in front of him of a Villa in Tuscany where his grandparents were born. He wanted to crawl inside the painting and be done with everything, but he loved Nicole too much to give up. Giving up, was not an option.

He mentally weighed the pros and cons of sending Rick to the diner. Mo was right, he hasn't met Nicole yet, but one day they would meet, and what if she recognized him as the man who had his eye on her one afternoon for no apparent reason? Still, the alternative, attempting to pull the truth from her lips, seemed like an impossible task – like a switch, she had shut herself off to him. She barely even looked at him and he had little faith that she would confide in him and seek comfort in his arms like she used to. Besides, Rick owed him one.

Swivelling back around, he told his friend, "Find him."

~

Michael sat at the bar, smoking one cigarette after another, and chasing down the nicotine with an icy cold beer. He nervously looked at the neon *Budweiser* clock next to the cash register. It was a quarter to five and there was no sign of Rick. Earlier, he had called home and Nicole rushed him off the phone, telling him that she was in the middle of feeding the baby. He expected her to ask him where he'd been all night, but she didn't, and her indifference made him even more nervous. He felt an ache in his heart. Underneath the muscles of his strong chest, his heart was fragile, just like everyone else.

Finally, Rick walked up to the bar and sat next to his boss. Jacob was standing in front of them, drying wine glasses.

"Leave us alone for a minute, kid."

"Sure, Mike."

When he was gone, he turned to Rick, impatiently.

"Well?"

"Nothing."

"What do you mean, *nothing?*"

"I didn't see anything. They talked."

"That's it? Was the baby there?"

"Yeah, Nicole was holding the baby the entire time."

The terror that filled Michael's chest cavity evaporated, just a little. "What else did you see?"

Rick shucked a peanut from its shell and popped it into his mouth, "Like I said, nothing. They didn't touch, and they didn't even laugh. It was more like a business meeting."

Mike wondered if this Edward guy owned a Daycare but that was kind of stupid seeing as most parents want to scope out the place where they'll be leaving their child. "What did he look like?"

"The guy?"

"Of course, the guy!"

"Okay, okay… calm down. He was older. He had grey hair and wore a suit."

"A suit."

"Yeah."

"Was he writing anything down?"

Rick thought hard, unaware that Michael was about to pounce on him, for taking his sweet time answering.

"Well!?"

"Um…I had to think…but yeah, he was writing stuff down. Do you want me to do anything else?"

"No," Mike said, staring at his empty mug.

"Okay, well, I'll go start my prep work."

Rick stood to make his way to the kitchen. He was pulling a double today, trying to make a little extra cash for his son's birthday party on the weekend. His wife wanted to hire a clown and although Rick said he could dress the part and save them some money, she stated the obvious and reminded him that their son would wonder where daddy was.

"Wait. What was she wearing?"

This question was easy to answer. Nicole was a beauty, that was for sure, and keeping his eyes on her for an hour was a job he could get used to.

"She was dressed casually. Jeans and a sweater."

Mike sighed, releasing the breath he had been holding for the last hour. "Thanks for doing this. I appreciate it."

"Anytime."

Rick started to walk away but Mike called out to him, motioning with his hand to return to the bar by tapping one finger on the dark lacquered wood. "If you tell anyone what happened today, you'll have to answer to me," Mike whispered.

"I get it. I won't say a word."

Michael nodded and when Rick was gone, he called Jacob over. "Cover me again tonight, kid."

"Is everything okay?"

"Yeah. I just have to get out of here. Tell Mo I'll call him later."

"No problem."

Michael pulled his coat from behind his bar stool and left the restaurant. In the back of the building, in the parking lot, he opened his car door, got inside, and slammed it against the reality he was facing. He still didn't know who the hell Edward was.

Starting the car, he put it in gear and drove steadily down the busy downtown streets, watching as huge snowflakes melted on his windshield. His hands gripped the steering wheel as if it were a life preserver. He pictured Nicole as he held her the night after making love for the first time, a few weeks after Stevie died.

Her head on his chest, she counted out the beats of his heart. She had told him, "888".

"That's how many beats you counted?"

"No, that's the number for infinity. I'll count forever."

"You should write a poem around that, baby."

"We just did."

Their lovemaking had been gentle, and they were careful to take it slow since Nicole was still in a delicate state – both in mind and in body. He knew he loved her before that. He knew he loved her the day he followed her when she set out to find Phelps. They had been lucky that day. When he woke in the hospital to learn that Phelps had died, and Nicole had survived, he felt the invisible shackles break away.

A few blocks from *Michael's Place*, he slid into an empty spot curbside to a store front. He had one other plan and he prayed to God that, this time, he would be able to get through to her. Without her, "infinity" made no sense.

Stepping out of the car, he walked up to the front door of *Regent Family Jewellers,* opened it, and walked inside, feeling instantly light-headed from all the damn lights shining over everything.

"Just in time," said an older man behind the counter, wearing a jeweller's loupe around his neck.

Michael shook the old man's hand and stared down at the navy blue, velvet box, he pulled from underneath the glass. The man had his hands on the box, but he didn't open it stretching out the anticipation – a move he's made on his customers since he started running the place in the 1950s. His father opened the doors in 1933 and *Regent's* was considered the best of the high-end jewellery stores in the city.

Slowly, he lifted the lid to the box exposing a two carat, flawless, round cut diamond, in a cathedral setting of 14K gold.

"Do you like?" the man asked in his thick Polish accent, a proud grin on his face.

Mike took the ring from its box and twirled it underneath the lights of the store. He was blinded by it. It almost matched the stars in Nicole's eyes that have grown dim lately, and he hoped that he could put the sparkle back. Looking the man dead in the eyes, he stated, "Sold."

"Excellent."

The jeweller put the box in the famous *Regent Family Jewellers* red bag and handed it to Mike who was holding out his Visa card. After running the card, he handed it back to Mike along with the slip and a pen. Michael signed his name for the purchase, once again shook the man's hand, and left the store. Across the street, he walked into *Cathy's Confectioneries*.

"Hey, Mike!"

Cathy greeted Michael in her usual way. She always felt like she had a hand in helping the romance between her employee and the handsome man before her blossom, and whenever she saw Michael, she still blushed like a schoolgirl. She wiped her hands on her white chef's coat and held them out to him. Michael took them and squeezed.

"Hi, Cathy."

"Well?" she said, taking back her hands. "Can I see it?"

"Sure," Mike told her, handing her the bag.

She quickly took the box from the bag, opened it and gasped. "Holy shit! It's huge!"

"Do you think she'll like it?"

Cathy's eyes were glued on the diamond. "If she doesn't, I'll take it!"

Michael managed to laugh. It felt good to laugh. "Is she coming?"

"Yup," Cathy informed him, handing the bag back to him. "I told her it was an emergency, and I would pay her cash if she helped me out tonight. I think it's super romantic what you're doing, Mike. I'm sure she'll love all of it."

Michael wasn't as confident that he could woo his wife back, but he was sure as hell going to try. After Mo and Rick left his office this afternoon, he sat alone, thinking. He thought of his Mamma and something she used to say. From a leaky faucet to a skinned knee, her answer was always the same: *L'amore ripara tutto. Love fixes everything.* Determined, he had called Cathy first, and then *Regent's.* He was paying Cathy to close the store tonight. He also gave Kim a head's up. As Maria's go-to babysitter, he had to make sure that she was available. He also made sure to ask her to keep Jacob in the dark until it was all over.

"Don't you worry about that! He doesn't even know what Santa's bringing the kids each year. That boy has a big mouth!" she said of her husband. *"But I love him,"* she added.

It was nearing half past five and Nicole would arrive for her pretend shift by six o'clock.

"You can hide in the back. Just give me five minutes and I'll be out of your hair."

"Thanks again, Cathy."

"No thanks, needed. You know I'm a sucker for romance. I'm curious though, what's the occasion?"

Michael wasn't sure that he wanted to disclose too much to Nicole's boss. In all sincerity, and without telling a lie, he said, "I just want her to know that I love her."

"Jesus, that's one lucky woman. Damn lucky, I'd say. I hope she knows that!"

From Cathy's lips, straight to Jesus' ears.

Fifteen

"Hey, baby."

Nicole walked into the bakery already wearing her white apron underneath her coat. She had dropped off Maria at Kim's who sported a wide grin on her face telling her it was put there by Christmas cheer. Nicole kissed Maria and set off to help her friend, welcoming the distraction of work.

She stood staring at her husband who was leaning on the glass of the cake display, his hands stuffed in the pockets of his jeans.

"Michael. What are you doing here? Where's Cathy?"

"She went home."

"Home? I thought she was going to the hospital to see her mother. Why are we here, Michael?"

"We need to talk."

"Why here, though?" she asked him, looking behind her at the door, still searching for Cathy.

"Come here," Mike told her, extending his hand.

Nicole stared at it. His eyes shone bright with love, a look she had memorized. She shook off her coat and threw it on a small two-seater next to the wall, and reached for Michael's hand and the minute he secured hers into his own, he pulled her into an embrace and squeezed the life out of her.

"God, it's so good to hold you, again."

"What's going on?" she asked, speaking into his chest. "You're scaring me."

He released her and looked into her eyes, both hands on the side of her face. "I've missed you, baby. I know you're scared about what's happening in this *Goddamn* city, but don't you know I'm here for you? Don't you!?" he repeated, shaking her head a little.

Finally, she pulled from his grasp and walked to the middle of the room.

"You're doing it again."

Spinning around, she challenged him. "Doing what?"

"Pulling away," he replied, sadly. "Why are you pulling away from me? I thought we were done with that shit!"

"Please don't raise your voice at me, Michael."

"I'm sorry. I am. I'm just so damn sick of this."

"Of what?"

"Of your rejection. Is this why we got married? So that we can live a life apart?"

"That's not it at all!"

"Well, what is it then?"

She walked over to one of the other small tables and sat down. Michael followed her, sitting across from her. *In the Air Tonight,* played on the radio and Mike waited, giving his wife the time she needed, and to give himself time to calm down. When she finally opened her mouth, it was like a gift.

"I went to see a psychiatrist, today."

Edward.

"Why, Nic?"

She pulled the apron over her head and draped it on the back of her chair. She played with the crucifix around her neck like he's seen her do a million times before; her attempt to seek God's help.

"Because Michael… I feel so lost."

"Even with me?"

"Especially *because* of you."

Sitting back, he crossed his arms over his heart. "What the hell does that mean?"

The empty ashtray before them tempted her. "Do you have a cigarette?"

"You don't smoke anymore."

"I just started again. Give me one, please."

Michael reached into the chest pocket of his baby blue button down and pulled a smoke from the package, lit it, and handed it to her. After lighting his own, he remembered, got up, and turned the sign on the door to "Closed" before locking them both inside.

Back at the table, he urged her to continue. "Please talk to me, baby."

Nicole remained quiet, gathering her thoughts, and staring at the tip of her smoke burning. Turning to him, she finally brought him with her to a time, twenty-years prior. "When I was little, I used to make fun of the other neighbourhood girls," she said, puffing awkwardly from her cigarette. "They would sit around on their porches playing *Barbies,* or *Go Fish,* or doing each other's hair. My mother used to urge me to join them, but I wanted nothing to do with them."

Michael fidgeted in his chair, feeling the sweat trickle down his back.

"I followed the boys, instead. They were a lot more fun," she admitted, smiling a little. "They went to the pond to fish, and rode their bikes too fast, and explored abandoned buildings. They let me tag along as long as I didn't say too much," she said, rolling her eyes at the memory.

"You were a thrill-seeker."

"Yeah. I was a tomboy, remember? Anyway, one day, we were on the train tracks. Just walking… to see where they would lead. That sort of thing."

Her long dark hair was up in a bun, exposing her beautiful face and Michael stared at her as if seeing her for the very first time.

"My shoelace came undone and got twisted around a rail joint while I was twirling and dancing, trying to make the boys notice me. I swear to you, Michael, when I heard that train whistle, it was the loudest noise I had ever heard, and would ever hear again. Instinctively, I panicked. I could have simply tried to take my shoe off but instead, I was intent on unravelling the lace from the joint."

Michael pictured the scenario in his mind, praising God that she was in front of him, able to tell him her story.

"All of the boys ran to safety, except one. I still remember his name. Christian. He told me not to move and to stop panicking and he took a Swiss Army knife from his pocket, sliced at a few laces, and helped me wriggle my foot free. The train passed moments later and as we sat in the grass, watching it go by, I knew then that I would one day marry a boy like Christian. You know what, Michael?"

"What?"

"I did. I married you."

She had put out her cigarette and Michael reached for her hand that still lingered on the table and held it. "So, what did you mean earlier then, baby? That you feel lost because of me?"

A Christmas carol took over the airwaves and Michael cringed, wishing Rudolph would fly into a meteor shower, and that the rock tunes would return.

"That day, I vowed to repay Christian somehow. Days and weeks passed and eventually, summer was over, and we went to different schools. I never saw him again. I never had a chance to repay him for what he did." She stared at the look of confusion on her husband's face. "I don't feel like I can ever repay you, Michael!"

Michael released her hand and stood abruptly, looking down at her. His voice stern, he yelled, "That's what you *think!?* That you have to repay me somehow!? For what?"

"For what? For saving my life that day!"

He smiled and shook his head back and forth, causing his bangs to fall over his eyes. Running his fingers through his hair, he tamed them back in place. "You can be so stupid sometimes, baby."

"Stupid!"

"Yeah, *stupid!*"

He went to her, descended on one knee, and grasped both

her hands. In between kissing them, he told her, "*You* saved *me*, too. Don't you know that? I'm lost without you, baby. You and Maria are my entire life and I need you but…" he said, growing emotional, "…more importantly, I *need* you to *want* me." The Bee Gees "How Deep is Your Love" filled the silence. Michael swallowed at the lump in his throat. His lips barely left her hands when he asked, "Do you…want me?"

She saw herself as she stood at Michael's bedside, two years ago on Christmas Eve.

They had sedated him, and his head and body were bandaged. A young doctor had told her that he had suffered severe second degree burns and that they didn't know the extent of the scarring that might ensue. Normally, the doctor explained to her, second degree burns only caused a change in the pigmentation of the skin, but Michael's burns bordered on third degree.

"How much of his body is affected?" Nicole asked her, crying.

"The left side of his face and ninety percent of the left side of his body. I'm sorry," the doctor said, impatient to leave and finish her rounds.

"For what?"

"Excuse me?"

"What are you sorry for? You said yourself that we're not sure about the extent of the scarring yet!"

"Please keep your voice down."

Nicole complied, seeking more information, "Is he in any pain?"

"He shouldn't be. The medication is pretty strong. I know this is difficult, but we can only give it time."

"We don't have time! He owns a Goddamn *restaurant!*"

"I asked you to keep your voice down, Miss."

Just then, Michael squeezed her hand as she held his good one. Even in pain, and unsure of how he might look once the burns healed, he was looking out for her.

The tears in her eyes spilled down her cheeks quietly until sobs overtook her, and then a crazy laughter emerged that helped unhinge all of the bad thoughts from a place deep in her mind. Michael still knelt beside her, pleading with her to answer him by not saying a single word. He was waiting for her, just like he always did.

"Jesus Christ, Michael, of course I want you."

"You do?"

"Of course," she repeated, running her hand down his face where the scarring was minimal. His left arm and leg were scarred the most. Seeing them made her want to crawl into herself and present parts of herself to him in trade. Giving him her heart, was the next best thing.

"I'm sorry if I did something to make you doubt that," she continued. "I'm sorry for everything…" She fell into his arms and in a voice, barely audible, she whispered, "Do you forgive me?"

"There's nothing to forgive, baby. Nothing."

Grasping the sides of both arms, he gently pushed her away from him. "We will get through this together. I promise. Do you believe me? Eh? Do you believe me, baby?" he asked her, rubbing his thumbs down both her cheeks.

Slowly, she nodded.

"Say it. Say that you believe me."

"I believe you."

Satisfied, he dropped his hands and stuffed one of them into his jeans' pocket.

"Good girl. This is for you, then," he told her, producing the velvet box.

"What's that?" she asked him, laughing.

Her laughter subsided when he opened the box and she saw a humongous diamond staring up at her. Her hand met her mouth and she looked at him, and then the ring, and then back at him, trying to decipher if both the man and the ring would disappear into thin air.

"It's…"

"Do you like it?"

"It's… incredible! I don't understand, though. I already have a ring," she told him, raising her hand.

"I know you do. This one goes on top," he said, taking the ring from her and sliding it on her ring finger. "And, young lady, I never want to see that you're not wearing it. Understood?"

"You don't have to ask me, twice," she told him, laughing again, unable to take her eyes off it.

He stood and took her hand so that she faced him, and he kissed her, fully, and with every ounce of his being. "We're okay, then?"

"I love you, Michael. Nothing will ever change that. I just…"

"Just what?" he asked, his insides churning.

"These recent murders… the memories. Just be patient with me."

"I am your husband, Nic. Besides being Maria's father, being your husband is the greatest honour I can think of. And one I don't take lightly. I love you, baby. I love you so much that it hurts sometimes."

She placed her head on his chest and wrapped her arms around his waist.

"Will you follow me?"

She nodded her head against his heart and with that one gesture, reaffirmed her trust in him.

Wordlessly, he led her across the room and behind the cash register, through a door that led to the bakery kitchen. He lifted her so that she sat on the wooden worktable. With his hands on her thighs, he kissed her at length. He moved his hands to the buttons on her white blouse and flicked at the top one and then the second, giving him room to slide his hand underneath her bra.

"Remember when I came here for Peaches, baby? To try and see you? You wouldn't give me the time of day, then."

His hand freed her breast from the cup of her bra and then he did the same to her other breast.

"I…remember," she managed to say, breathless from desire.

"You drove me mad that day, baby."

He fully unbuttoned her blouse and released her arms from it. He reached behind her back and unclasped her bra, pulling the straps from her shoulders. "Are you okay?" he whispered in her ear, unwilling to hurt her.

She signaled to him that she was, and he bit gently at her lobe, reaching for the button on her jeans and pulling at her zipper. "Lift your bottom," he ordered.

Sliding the jeans over her legs, he pulled them off and dropped them to the floor, along with her socks. She inched her fingers towards the buttons of his shirt, but he grasped both of her wrists and held them against her naked thighs, kissing her deeply.

"I thought I would lose my mind that day," he confessed. "I wanted you from the first time I saw you. Did you know that?"

She managed to nod, picturing the mysterious man whose mission it was to make her his.

Michael pulled at her underwear by crooking one finger in the waistband and sliding them down her legs. Gently, he guided her body along the length of the table and climbed the counter hovering over her. She was fully naked, while he was fully clothed. She arched her back, searching for him but he continued to tease her, causing her desire to grow until she ached.

"Michael…"

"Quiet."

He grazed her mouth, gently at first, and then bit at her bottom lip, and finally, thrust his tongue inside her mouth, meeting hers – a discussion without words.

"I always knew you'd be mine, Nic," he admitted, coming up for air.

He kissed her neck, her chest, and then took her breast in his mouth. He slid his tongue along her flat stomach, kissing every inch of her. He stopped abruptly, intentionally trying to drive her insane.

Nicole pulled his head back down, and he resumed the exploration of her body, running one hand over her hip and around her back until he found her cheek and he squeezed, hard.

"I always knew we were meant to be together."

"I…"

"Shh!"

Her hands ran through his hair, and she moaned a plea for him to take her, but he continued to plague her with the most delicious torture. When she couldn't resist any longer, she called his name with a growl, *"Michael!"*

Within seconds, his hands met his belt and when he was free, he entered her, watching with pleasure as she writhed unapologetically, and she connected with him in the exact way he had hoped for, a way that mimicked his own: one that spoke of pure and utter abandon.

Sixteen

"Come on Stacy. One more for the road."

"You said that an hour ago! I'm leaving. Besides, I have to set up early for the office potluck in the morning."

"Don't you usually have your Christmas party at night?"

"Not this year. Keith is cutting corners. I better go."

"You're no fun."

"And you guys party too hard!" she said over the roar the house band, *The Crystals.*

Stacy made her way through the crowded pub ignoring a drunk guy who tried to pick-up her up by using some cheesy line on her. He was kind of cute underneath his beer-induced stupor, but she wasn't interested.

"Not tonight, sailor," she told him laughing.

Outside, she faced the night air as if hitting an invisible wall. The wind was fierce, and she pulled her scarf further around her face. She lived only a few blocks from the pub but with the biting cold, it felt like miles. Picking up her pace, she thought about the report that was due tomorrow for her boss, Keith, who liked to go through her work with a microscope, pointing out even the slightest spelling mistake. She felt humiliated, like a school kid does when told to colour within the lines. She was looking for another job, but with Christmas coming, no one was hiring and she was stuck with him until at least the new year.

The streets were relatively empty. It was late, and the weather caused everyone to stay home.

At the street corner, she waited for the walk signal and without warning, she thought of her ex-boyfriend, Robert. They had broken up only a week earlier. She was the one to end it and she could see his heart breaking through his *Pink Floyd* t-shirt. He had asked her what he had done, and he told her that he could change but the truth of the matter was that she simply wasn't attracted to him. She sought fire, and his love burned more like a matchstick.

A wicked wind made her hold her hood down with one hand, some blonde tendrils escaping from underneath. "Come on, you stupid light."

Finally, she gave up waiting and looked both ways before crossing. With her hair whipping around her, and the hood covering half of her face, she didn't see the black sedan that almost ran her over. She was pulled backwards, back onto the sidewalk, and lost her balance. A man helped her up.

"Are you okay?"

"God, that was close. Thank you."

"You should be more careful."

She could smell booze on his breath as it danced on the wind in her direction. She nodded and dusted the snow off her coat. Finally, the light changed, and she moved forward, carefully, this time. Her boots clicked on the sidewalk, and slightly out of rhythm, she could hear a different set of boots behind her. The man was following her. *Stop being paranoid, Stace. You're not the only one who lives downtown,* she told herself. Still, she walked faster, and the click of her heels was matched with the thud of the man's boots. *Jesus,* she whispered, quietly. She turned around briefly, and he was staring straight at her. Looking in front of her, she tried to find an open coffee shop or video store, but it was past midnight. Suddenly, she was hit from behind as if she was walking on a crowded New York City sidewalk. Spinning on her heel, she saw him standing there, smiling, his hands deep in his coat pockets.

"What do you want?"

"Just making sure you get home safe," he said, still smiling.

"Well, I'm fine, okay? Good night."

She turned from him, panicking inside, and veered to her right to take a short-cut through the park. She didn't usually take the short-cut at night. There were very few lights on in the park, but the sooner she could get home, the sooner she could jump in bed and visit Never Never Land.

She looked over her shoulder, and the man was gone. Breathing a sigh of relief, she made a mental note to talk to the girls about sharing a cab next time they went out together. The snow was deeper in the park, which was another reason she avoided it. Her new leather boots would ruin, and she cursed the weirdo who caused her to take this route.

Suddenly, out of nowhere, he stepped out in front of her. The scream left her lungs in a grey muffled vortex, and he grabbed her and cupped his leather-gloved hand over her mouth.

"Scream again, I'll snap your neck. Do you understand?"

Her head felt like it was in a vice, but she managed to nod, her eyes wide with terror.

Still holding her, he released his hand from her mouth and grabbed a handful of her hair. His knee met her stomach, forcing her to double over. Pushing her the rest of the way to the ground, her face in the snow, he kept one knee on her back and tore the hood from her head. He reached into his inside coat pocket and snapped open a pocketknife. Grasping her hair in a ponytail, he sawed away at it as she screamed and cried into the snow.

Freezing rain fell upon them, which made him happy since it would disguise them, and muffle her attempts to call for help. He'd have to hurry with this one, though.

As he turned her over, she looked up at him and pleaded for her life. *"Please.* Please, I'll do anything. Just don't hurt me."

"What makes you think you can ask me for anything? Eh?"

"I…"

"Answer me, you *slut.*" He leaned over her; his face inches form hers so that she could see the spaces between his teeth. He still held her hair in his hand, and he shoved it in her face and then tossed it to the side. Her whimpers and cries annoyed him – it was like static in his ears.

The freezing rain fell harder. It was loud, and it was then that he took his knife, ripped open her coat, and cut through the material of her blouse.

"No, *please!*"

"Shut the hell up!"

To make sure she'd comply, he swiped the knife across her lips, and then her neck, finally silencing her.

Placing the tip of the knife blade at her navel, he dug in using a circular pattern. He liked to disfigure their bodies in different ways. *Normal, is boring* – that was his motto. He watched, amused, as the snow around her turned a deep red. Gathering a handful, he stuffed it in her mouth.

It was time for his signature move and like a veteran surgeon, he pulled the eye from her socket, cleanly and expertly. Satisfied with his work, he turned and walked away, whistling *Jingle Bells.*

Seventeen

"...police have confirmed the identity of the murder victim, as twenty-three-year-old, Stacy Rodman. Police have also verified that, like the pervious two victims, Miss Rodman's eye had been extracted, making them attribute the murders to a serial killer that has been deemed by the press as a copy-cat killer, alluding to the infamous Stevie Phelps case..."

Mo quickly switched the knob on the radio to the off position when he saw Michael enter the kitchen.

"Hey, I was listening to that!" Mario yelled from across the room where he stood at his station prepping the butter for the garlic bread.

"No, you weren't. Get to work."

"I *am* working!"

Michael stared between them, "What's going on?"

"Nothing, Mike. The Baccala is next to the sink." "Thanks."

Michael made his way over to the sink where a huge tub of cod fish lay underwater. The traditional Christmas Eve Italian favourite would be on the menu for the rest of the month.

"How long's it been?"

"Only 34 hours."

Michael dipped one finger in the tub and put the tip in his mouth tasting salt, but only vaguely. Generally, it took three days underwater before the fish released its preservation salt.

"Let's change the water now and keep a watch on it. Should be okay in another day."

"Got it," Mo said, walking over to him. Lowering his voice, he asked him, "How did it go yesterday?"

Mike patted him on the shoulder. "Not here. Come to my office."

Once safely inside Michael's office, he told Mo, "Edward is a psychiatrist."

"That's what Rick said?"

"No, Nic told me. I feel like an ass for even sending Rick to spy on her."

"It could have gone either way. It could have been anyone. Does this mean you two are talking again?"

Michael felt his insides warm as he thought of their lovemaking yesterday. His lips still tingled and yet, he longed to hold her.

Before leaving the bakery, they grabbed two Peaches out of the fridge and left Cathy a note of thanks along with money that they left in an envelope in the cash register. At home, after making sure that Kim was okay to keep the baby overnight, Michael made a quick sauce, and they ate spaghetti by candlelight and devoured the Italian dessert that looked like peaches by feeding them to one another. He had kissed some lingering cream off her lips, reminding him of their wedding day when he did the same with a cake that she had made herself. Afterwards, they cuddled on the couch and watched Nicole's favourite Christmas movie, "It's a Wonderful Life" until sleep overtook her, and he carried her upstairs and tucked her into bed, placing the covers over her nose the same way she did every night. He spoke to her in his mind, telling her that he loved her, and lied down next to her, searching for her ring underneath the covers. She had kept her promise and wore it to bed. Despite the anxiety he still felt regarding the recent murders, he was able to sleep soundly.

"Yeah. We're talking," he said, grinning.

"Glad to hear it. Do you think Rick will keep his mouth shut?"

"He better. But yeah, I do."

"Well, all's well that ends well, as they say."

"When the hell did you turn British?"

"Shut up."

Mo looked at his watch and stood to leave to cover Jacob at the bar for his break. At the door, he turned back around, "Hey, Mike?"

"Yeah."

"What if there's more from this copy-cat killer. Will she be okay?"

"I hope so, *Amico Mio*."

Mo nodded and left, shutting the door behind him. Walking across the dining room, he mumbled, *I hope so too. For everyone's sake.*

~

It was a slow night and Mike had sent both Mo and Jacob home as thanks for covering for him the last few days. The weather was still wreaking havoc on the city and only a few tables were occupied at *Michael's Place.*

Mike stood behind the bar, aware of the guy sitting next to a lone woman. He stared at her every so often and by his fifth gin and tonic, he didn't try to hide the lust that was apparent on his face. She was a woman in her late forties with shoulder length brown hair, wearing a red dress that tied at the waist. She had a silhouette that could compete with Sophia Loren's and kind, matronly eyes. Sipping on her second glass of red wine, she nibbled on a classic white pizza.

"My compliments to the chef," she told Mike who stood in front of her slicing lemons.

"You just complimented him."

"This is your creation? *Fantastico!*" she said kissing her fingers.

He grinned from ear to ear. "Chef" was the third title attributed to his name and he was proud of it. Like his parents, he considered the food to be the most important part of the restaurant. Otherwise, it was just a place to store tables and chairs.

"Hey, lady," the man next to her said, slurring his words.

He wore a suit, but his tie was undone and the crooked features on his face lacked refinement, as if he were a bum playing dress-up.

"Can I help you?" she asked him, turning in her bar stool.

"Can I buy you a drink?"

"I already have a drink, thank you," she swivelled back around and rolled her eyes at Mike who was listening to every word.

"Aww, come on doll-face. It's Christmas!" the man said, finishing his drink.

"I said that I'm *fine*, thank you."

"Hey, bartender. A refill for me and a glass of wine for the lady."

Michael walked a few steps over to where the man was sitting, picked up his glass, and placed it in the nearby sink.

"What are you doing? I said I wanted a refill."

"You're cut off."

"What? Why?"

"Because I said so," Mike told him, leaning with both hands on the bar.

"I wanna speak with management."

Smirking, Mike informed him, "I *am* management and I reserve the right to refuse service to rude assholes like you. Go home."

The woman stared at them until she met the eyes of her would-be suitor.

"You're a tease, you know that?"

"Excuse me?"

"Yeah. I saw you staring at me and now you pretend you don't know what I mean."

"I was *not* staring at you."

"Get out of here, buddy. *Now*," Michael said, leaning further over the bar. "And don't come back."

The man turned his head swiftly towards Michael, "You're banning me?"

"Yeah. What of it?"

Lost for words and clearly drunk, the man rose from his bar stool, cursing audibly. "Big mistake, buddy."

"Oh yeah?"

"Yeah."

"Well, I guess I'm off *Santa's Nice List*, then. Get out."

"*Stupid bitch...*" the guy mumbled.

"What did you call her?"

"A stupid *bitch!*"

Without bothering to walk around the bar, Michael reached over and grabbed the man from the shirt collar. "If I ever see your lousy face in here again, I'll mangle it for you. No charge."

"This is assault!"

"No," Michael told him, losing his patience, and raising his fist. "This is."

"Wait!" the woman said, desperate to stop a fight.

The other diners in the room stared at the scene but Michael stood frozen in place, his fist still in the air.

"I'm okay. Just make him leave."

"You sure, lady? Because I really don't mind using his face as a punching bag."

"I'm sure. I'm *sure!*"

Michael let go of the man who stumbled backwards. "You're lucky she has more class than you ever will. Get the hell out."

Wordlessly, the man picked up his briefcase from where it sat on the floor and left. As if nothing happened, Mike went back to slicing his lemons.

"Thank you," he heard the woman say.

"No need to thank me. That guy was an ass. Your dinner is on me, tonight."

"Again, thank you."

The woman sat quietly looking at Michael. She could count every muscle defined through his dress shirt. His sleeves rolled up, she noticed the scars on his left arm, and they added an air of mystery to the man who exuded sexiness without even trying. She looked around her. The other diners resumed eating and the scene was forgotten. It was a quiet nod to the respect bestowed upon on the owner of *Michael's Place* and the woman was intrigued.

"If it had been you offering to buy me that drink..." Michael looked up to see her staring at him over the rim of her wine glass. "I'm married."

"Oh, your ring is on the..."

"Wrong hand, I know."

"Your wife is lucky to have you."

"I'm the one who's lucky," Michael told her, refilling her wine glass for her. Chivalry, she realized, was not dead. It was wounded.

"You know...my Domenic used to say that about me," she stated, her eyes glistening.

"Your husband?"

"Yes. He died last year. God rest his soul."

"I'm really sorry to hear that."

She shrugged a little and raised her eyebrows as if to say: *What can you do?*

"You get used to it after a while. It's like they become some sort of character you once read about in a novel. They're still there, but not really. You do whatever it takes."

"Whatever it takes?"

"To mend your heart."

"Mr. Rossi, they need you in the kitchen."

Michael's waitress, Stephanie, was standing a few feet from them, a breadbasket in each hand.

"Thanks, I'll be right there," he told her. Turning to the woman again, he was surprised to see her putting on her coat.

"You know that guy was a jerk, right?"

"I know," she said, pulling a twenty-dollar bill from her wallet.

"Please...it's on me, really."

"Oh this? This isn't for you. It's for the chef," she told him, winking.

She put her coat on but didn't button it. Taking her purse and leather gloves from the bar, she left without another word.

Michael picked up the money and her wine glass. A business card fell to the floor that she had pulled out along with the cash. Curious, Mike turned it over: *"Julia Regina, 596-9865. Elite Escort."*

Whatever it takes.

Eighteen

Nicole sat at home at the kitchen table mindlessly flipping through a magazine, the baby monitor in front of her. She had just hung up the phone after speaking with her mother. She invited her parents to visit them for Christmas informing her that she and Michael would pay the airfare from Saskatchewan as their Christmas gift. Her mother declined the offer, telling her daughter that it was difficult for Nicole's father to get around since his knee surgery. It was an excuse, she knew, and she wiped at her eyes with her shirt sleeve.

Her parents had yet to meet their granddaughter. They haven't even met Michael yet, and the anger that bubbled up inside of her turned to sadness. Her mother didn't suggest that they fly to Saskatchewan, giving credence to what Nicole had always believed: her parents were indifferent towards her. Like a domino effect, their disdain for each other trickled down to her.

She wondered why it was that they even bothered pretending anymore. Ever since Nicole was a little girl, she could sense that her parents hated each other. There were no public displays of affection, no birthday celebrations, or anniversaries to commemorate. When Nicole was old enough to live on her own, she got the hell out, and moved across several provinces to get away from them. There was nothing stopping them from divorcing except, maybe, the fact that they were older and simply didn't want to bother with lawyers, paperwork, and finding new places to live.

Her parents met later in life on a flight from Germany. Her mother was a Stewardess, and her father was an accountant who had been visiting family overseas. They were married after only three months and three months after that, they learned that they were pregnant with Nicole.

It was a common enough story, but maybe that was the problem. "Common" is not the stuff that fairy tales are made of. To her parents, passion is defined by cheering for the same football team on Sundays and even then, they will quiet each other, even during commercials, and make their own snacks ignoring one another in the kitchen. They lived like roommates and the charming Prince stayed within the pages of the storybook still searching for Cinderella's slipper.

Nicole sighed and got up to fill her coffee cup. She wasn't looking forward to telling Michael that her parents had dismissed them once again. Maria would grow up without grandparents since both of Michael's parents had already passed away. She was sick of trying with them. Her mother had even rushed her off the phone, even though Nicole assured her that she would be picking up the long-distance charges.

The baby monitor came to life with the sound of Maria's cries. Putting down her cup, Nicole ascended the stairs of their two-story home and went to her daughter. Picking up her warm little body, it was the best therapy she could imagine. She held the baby against her heart and smelled the sweetness of her hair. "You and your father are *everything* to me," she whispered.

She sat with the baby in the rocking chair to lull her for a few minutes. She thought of Michael and her heart leapt as if being shocked with a defibrillator. She loved everything about him – from his sexy good looks to his protective nature, to his unwavering loyalty. He worked hard to be able to support his family, and his generosity and kindness were apparent in every action, like the time he had made an anonymous donation to the Children's Hospital using the money he was saving to buy himself a new car. *"Old one takes me from A to B,"* he explained to her when she asked him why he did it. *"The kids need it more."* He was able to dismiss nonsense by cocking a single eyebrow and others respected him. Above all else, he loved her deeply.

Setting the baby back in her crib, Nicole made her way

back downstairs to prepare a bottle. She harbored a secret from her husband and despite knowing that she could trust him with her life, she still felt trapped. Her fear was like a noose and no one, not even Michael, could release her from it.

She opened the cupboard above the sink and reached for the prenatal vitamins she used to take. Opening the cap, she poured two pills into the palm of her hand. They weren't vitamins. She had flushed them down the toilet and discarded the brown bottle that housed the pills she was about to take by throwing it in a trash can on the sidewalk. She had peeled the label off and thrown the bottle away, feeling like a fraud. She quickly rinsed her coffee cup, filled it halfway with water from the tap, and swallowed the two pills, putting the bottle back in the cupboard in full view. They weren't vitamins, but Michael would never know the difference.

Nineteen

Detective Valetti poured Ray a shot from a bottle of Scotch into a Styrofoam cup and put the bottle back in his bottom desk drawer. He got up to stand at his office window, surveying the half-empty precinct. His assistant was at her desk, eating a sandwich of some sort and he turned the blinds to prevent her from peering into his office. Back at his desk, he pushed an ashtray towards his colleague who held the ever-present cigar between his fingers.

"What do you got for me?"

Ray slid a report across the desk towards his friend and picked up his cup, swallowing the alcohol in one gulp. A photograph was paper clipped to the report. The mutilated body of the young woman made Valetti's stomach lurch. It never got any easier and he envisioned what she might have looked like before the murder robbed her of her beauty.

Ray watched as Valetti scanned the report, his one eye bopping over the words. A scowl invaded his features until finally, Sam took his own cup, drank from it, and threw it a few feet away where it landed on the floor next to the garbage can.

"That's it?"

"That's it."

"*Dammit!* What the hell is going on with forensics?"

"Don't shoot the messenger."

Sitting back in his chair, his hands over his protruding stomach, Valetti absorbed the information, or lack of information, rather.

"What about the hair? Can't they analyze the hair?"

"They did. Negative."

Sam picked up a pen from his desk and chewed on it until his teeth hurt. Ray reached over and picked up the report, looked at it and then placed it in Sam's line of vision, his finger over one sentence.

"See this?"

Miss Rodman's bottom lip was found several inches to the left of her neck; the top lip was found one inch to the right of it.

"Yeah, so?"

"It doesn't mention her eye, Sam. They usually find the eyeball somewhere near the victim."

Sam took the report and put it up to his face, as if the action would help the words materialize. "It's nowhere in the report?"

"Nada."

"So, where the hell is it then? Did they do a thorough search?"

"They did the usual search."

"Well, for *Christ sakes*, that's not good enough anymore! Where's Constantine? I want to talk to him."

"Gone for the day."

"This is a *Goddamn* murder investigation! What do you mean he's gone for the day?"

"It's pretty late Sam. I can vouch for the guy. He's been here since four this morning."

Sam looked at the clock on his desk. It was eight o'clock at night and he had forgotten to call Elise and tell her he wouldn't be home for dinner again. He wondered why she hadn't called him to check up on him, but she was probably having tea with the neighbour, an older woman that Elise liked to play cards with. Sam sighed and stared at the cup Ray was holding. "Drink?" he asked his friend.

"Sure," Ray replied, pushing his cup forward.

"Not here. Let's get out of here."

"Where to?"

"I don't care," he told him, walking over to the hook by the door and putting his scarf on and then his coat. "Wait. On second thought, I know where… and dinner is on me."

~

"What do you mean, it's a thirty-minute wait? I'm starving!"

Sam eyed the young girl who stood at the hostess desk at *Michael's Place.* The restaurant was full. Coaches, parents, and kids from a minor hockey team were celebrating their latest win. Several other tables were already reserved and nothing Sam could say would get him and Ray seated any faster. Then he remembered he was supposed to ask for Michael when he returned for his free dinner.

"Where's your boss?"

"Mr. Rossi is at the bar. Would you like to speak with him?"

Sam looked at his friend and then at the young girl. He kept his voice down, but his tone was firm, "If I didn't want to speak with him, I wouldn't have asked you where he was."

"I'll get him for you."

"Much obliged," he told her, sarcastically.

A few minutes later, Michael was at the hostess station.

"Can we get a table, or what?"

Michael recognized the one-eyed man and his friend, and he wished that they would both disappear and take their air of superiority with them. He was a man of his word, however, and he owed them at least one dinner.

"I'll take it from here, Sylvia. Thank you."

"Okay, Mr. Rossi."

"Sylvia, wait. Can you please ask Jacob to change the radio station?"

"Sure thing, sir."

The girl walked away shyly. Her face reddened every time Michael spoke to her. She was young, and she had yet to go on a date. She wasn't interested in boys yet, but even she could sense that her boss was unlike any boy she would ever meet. The older waitresses were constantly talking about him in the ladies' room where they all stood around smoking on their breaks. One girl had called Michael *way harsh*, and that she wouldn't mind *penciling him in* if his wife ever *hit the dirt*.

The smoke of the cigar that one of the men was holding was making Michael sick.

"*I Saw Mommy Kissing Santa Claus* ain't your thing?"

"Not really, no. Here for your free dinner?"

"No, we're here for the music."

Ray stifled a laugh while Michael just stood there. "Well?"

"We're full. Eat at the bar or you'll have to wait."

Valetti turned to his friend who simply shrugged. "We'll eat at the bar."

"Follow me," Michael told them both.

At the bar, he asked Jacob to pick up two table settings from the kitchen. Mo was busy with other patrons who occupied the remaining bar stools. They were indulging in spirits, using the Holiday Spirit as their go-to reason.

"What's your poison?"

"Scotch for me."

"I'll take a beer," Ray told Michael.

"Bottle or draft?"

"Draft."

Michael left to pour a draft of beer, mumbling under his breath. The one-eyed guy was trying his patience, but he kept his cool for the sake of the other diners, especially the kids who did everything by example and if Michael threw the guy out by his shirt collar without cause, he'd look like a bully, and bullying was not okay – at any age.

Carrying the mug of beer over to Ray, he set it down, grabbed a rock glass, and put two ice cubes in it.

"Neat," Sam said.

"What?"

"Neat, no ice."

Keeping his eyes on Sam, Michael poured the ice out of the glass by turning it upside down over the floor. He grabbed a bottle of Scotch by reaching behind him, his eyes still focused in front of him. Pouring a shot, he placed the bottle down.

"A double."

Ray watched, amused, and puffed from his cigar, quietly.

Again, Michael raised the bottle and poured a second shot into Sam's glass and then put a menu in front of each man. Jacob was back with the place settings and arranged napkins and cutlery in front of the men, as well as a pair of salt and pepper shakers.

"Thanks, kid. Wait for their orders. Comp one dinner. I'll be in my office if you need me."

"No problem, Mike."

Michael began to walk away, aware that Valetti was watching him.

"Michael."

He stopped and turned. "What?"

"You owe me one lunch and one dinner."

Walking back over to the man, he asked him, "So? It's dinner time, isn't it?"

"How about we say my friend here gets his meal for free, and I'll skip the lunch."

Michael's insides rattled but the sooner he was rid of them, the better. "Fine." Turning to Jacob, he told him, "Comp both dinners. They pay for the alcohol."

"Got it, boss."

Michael walked to his office and slammed the door shut. He quickly lit a smoke and picked up his office phone. He dialed home and waited. By the tenth ring, he was about to jump out of his skin when Nicole answered, breathless.

"You were busy?"

"Yeah. I just finished putting Maria down."

"Is everything okay?"

"Yes. I miss you, though," she told him, tenderly.

"I miss you, too."

"Are you closing tonight?"

"Yeah. I'll be home after midnight."

"Okay. My parents aren't coming again," she stated flatly.

Michael cringed. He knew how much Nicole longed for her parents to visit and he hated them for hurting her.

"I'm sorry, Nic. We don't need them. We'll have our own Christmas, okay?"

He waited until there was life across the airwaves. "Okay."

"Lock the door, baby."

"It's already locked."

"I love you."

"I love you, too. Drive safe."

Michael hung up and cursed out loud. His wife's parents were the opposite of his own. His heart ached imagining his mother holding their daughter with love and pride, showing the baby off to all her friends. His heart hurt, envisioning his pop bouncing Maria on his knee, his granddaughter giggling with glee. Both things would never happen, and he detested the Hartes for giving up their chance to make the vision come to life. He wished that Nicole would stop grieving them. There is nothing worse than grieving the loss of someone who is still alive.

Michael lit another smoke and grabbed a pile of papers from his inbox. He didn't normally do payroll when the restaurant was packed but he'd rather sit in his office and hide. He wanted to get away from the scrutiny coming from the man with one eye. There was something else that he hated, and the one-eyed man liked to throw it around like confetti: arrogance.

~

An hour and a half later, Michael left his office closing the door behind him. All the tables in the place were now occupied, and the noise in the restaurant overpowered the music. One man was standing at a round table of eight making a toast. A man at a table for two was holding his lady's hand across the linen, as if he was about to propose. The hockey kids were gathered around the pool tables and one kid looked like he was trying to channel Paul Newman from *The Hustler*.

Behind the bar, Michael adjusted the volume on the stereo system by turning it up a notch. Jacob walked up next to him and nudged him in the ribs. "They haven't eaten yet."

"Who?" Michael asked, turning to stare at him.

Jacob cocked his head to the left and Michael looked over his shoulder. The one-eyed guy was motioning with his hands, swinging his drink back and forth causing Scotch to slosh from it.

"How many drinks has he had?"

"That's his fourth. All doubles."

"Jesus, kid. Why didn't you cut him off?"

Jacob took a smoke from the package that sat beside the stereo and placed a cigarette behind his ear. "The other one is sober. That's only his second beer. Said he'd take care of his friend. I think they're celebrating something."

Michael sighed heavily. "I'll take over."

"Thanks, Mike. He's talking really weird."

"About what?"

"He's rambling on about weird stuff."

"What *kind* of stuff?"

"You'll see," Jacob told him, walking away to serve a customer who sat further down the bar with his hand raised.

Michael grabbed Mo's arm as he walked by and took a stack of napkins from the tray he was carrying.

"I was going to fold those."

"I got it. Take a break."

"Thanks, Mike."

He stood in front of the two men, folding napkins just a bit too slowly. Neither man looked at him and he strained to listen to one-eyed-guy, who was doing most of the talking.

"I read it in Time magazine," he was saying.

"Come on, Sam."

"It's true. In some cases, the dead person has no clue that they're dead."

"Which cases might that be?"

"I don't know! Cases."

Ray shook his head and finished the last of the peanuts that sat in front of him.

"Imagine," Valetti continued, sipping from his glass, "what a shitty morning that would be? You would be talking to your wife, or boss, or the gal who serves you coffee, and they don't answer you. You think they're ignoring you but really, you're not there. You just imagine you are. Imagine?"

He drained his glass and finally noticed Michael standing in front of him, behind the bar. "Another."

Michael looked at Ray who nodded.

"You just said the word imagine three times, Sam."

"So? That's not the point, is it Ray?"

Michael poured another double into the glass of the one named Sam. The kid had been right. In all his years standing behind a bar, Michael had never heard anyone talk about death like this guy, as if it was fun.

"Imagine," he repeated, "that you're just pumping away at your wife," he said, laughing uncontrollably, "and she doesn't move or moan or nothin'!"

Ray stood from his stool. "I'm going for a piss."

"You do that!" Sam called after him.

"They're not worth it, you know," Sam said in Mike's general direction.

"Who's not worth it?"

"Broads. Wives."

Michael looked at the man's hand where his wedding ring glinted underneath the bar lights. "I'm sure your wife would love to hear that."

Sam smirked and drained his glass. "Another."

"Don't you think you've had enough?"

"You keepin' count?"

"It's my job to keep count."

"Oh yeah? How many you at?"

"Five doubles, apparently."

"And countin'. Just pour the damn drink."

Michael eyebrows knitted but he poured him another drink, stating, "That's your last one."

"Or what? You'll have me arrested?" Sam laughed again, unable to control the cough that accompanied it.

Another patron to his right stared at him. A young man wearing a ball cap and drinking from a bottle of *Blue*. "What's so funny about that?" the young man asked him.

"Huh?" Sam grunted, turning slightly in his chair.

"What's so funny about getting arrested?"

"What's it to you?"

"Just wondering what your train of thought is," the kid said, an open textbook in front of him.

Michael stood quietly, one napkin in his hand. Despite the absurdity of the topic, he was curious to hear what Sam had to say.

"Irony!"

"Irony?"

"Yeah, irony!" Sam pulled at his sport coat, victoriously showing his badge. "You have I.D. on you, kid? Because it looks to me like you're not old enough to shave, let alone drink."

The young man slapped his book shut so that Michael could read the title, *Canadian Law*. He quickly stood from his stool and made his way out of the restaurant.

"Great," Michael mumbled, tossing the napkin down. Retrieving the bottle of beer, he poured the rest of it down the sink.

"You do ask for I.D. here, don't you, *Michael?*"

Ray was back from the restroom and listened to Sam as he went on another verbal rampage.

"You do know that it's the *law*, don't you? You do know that it's illegal to serve alcohol to people who are underage?"

"Yeah," Mike answered, unflinching. "We ask for I.D."

"Are you sure? Seems like that kid couldn't wait to make his get-away."

"Look, finish your drink and go home."

"That's what I thought," Sam said, satisfied. "Kid looked like he'd enjoy a ride on a *Goddamn* carousel."

Michael was standing with his hands in his jeans pockets, and he pulled them out to lean over the bar.

"What did you just say?"

"Which part?"

"The *last* part."

Suddenly, Sam's face relaxed into something serious. The Scotch was pooled in his bloodshot eye. He observed Michael as if he was in his interrogation room back at the precinct, but Michael stood his ground waiting for an answer.

"Nothing," Sam finally said, finishing his drink and trying to stand without falling over.

"Where are you going?"

"Home."

"What about your free dinner?"

"I guess you still owe me one."

"Yeah," Michael said, taking his hands off the bar. "Come back anytime," he said, cheerfully.

"Let's go, Ray."

"Sam, is it?" Michael asked, stopping the man.

"You're a smart one, Michael. What do you want?"

"How'd you lose that eye?"

"Come on, Sam, let's go," Ray prodded.

"Hold on a second," then turning to Michael, his smile returned. "Why do you want to know?"

"Just curious."

The detective mimicked Mike and leaned on the bar, purposefully leaving his sport coat open as if advertising his job by keeping his badge in full view.

"I don't kiss and tell on the first date, friend. See you next time. You can tell me about your scars," he said, winking.

After the two men left, Michael noticed Jacob standing next to him.

"See? Weird, eh?"

"Yeah, kid. And he was a cop."

The word *carousel* reverberated in Michael's ears.

"So?"

Michael paused, contemplating what just happened. The one-eyed man had alluded to the one thing that had a hand in changing Michael's and Nicole's lives and he wanted to know why, of all the rides in the world, he would speak of the merry-go-round.

"Let's help Mo close up shop, here," he told Jacob who was standing there with a bar towel in his hands.

Michael strode away, and Jacob literally scratched at his head. It had been a strange night, one that could compete with Jacob Marley's.

Suddenly, Mike was back, and he stood before him, "And kid?"

"Yeah, boss."

"Remember to check Goddamn I.D. next time, would you?"

"What do you mean?"

"The kid drinking *Blue.* He was underage."

"Oh. Yeah, sure. Sorry, Mike."

There was no kid drinking *Blue.* Not one that Jacob had served, at least. Must have been the ghost of his namesake, Marley, who planted the beer. A strange night, indeed.

Twenty

All the lights were on at the Valetti household, save for the lights on the Christmas tree which stood proud at the living room window that faced the street.

Valetti looked at his watch and gulped. It was a quarter to one in the morning and the last time he spoke with Elise was this morning at eight before heading to the precinct.

He blew his breath into one hand and smelled it. There'd be no hiding the Scotch on his breath.

Steadying himself, he unlocked the front door after several tries and entered the house, tripping on the welcome mat at his feet. Four suitcases sat in the foyer and Elise stood in front of him, wearing her Winter coat, hat, and gloves.

"Did you have a nice night, Sam?"

"Elise, what's the meaning of this?"

Her hands were crossed in front of her, and her face was cross with a look of disgust. "I'm going on a trip."

"What kind of trip?" he asked her, moving forward but hitting the wall beside him. It seemed like it was falling on him and not the other way around. The entire room swayed, and he struggled to maintain control.

"I'm going to spend Christmas with my sister in Nova Scotia."

"Christmas! What about me?"

"What about you, Sam!?"

Elise had only ever raised her voice to her husband a half-dozen times during their entire marriage and the sound of it made his head spin.

"What about you?" she repeated. "Does drinking come

with the job, now?"

"I wasn't drinking," he stupidly said, slurring his words.

"I'm not going to live like this anymore," she told him, shaking her head.

"Like what?"

"Like I'm an officer's widow!" A look of pure sadness shadowed her face. "You didn't even bother to call me today."

Valetti took another step forward, but his wife raised her hand in front of her like a crossing guard. "Stop. Stop right there, Sam."

"Elise. Honey. You know I'm working on a case, and…"

"I can't hear you. I can't hear you anymore through your excuses. I'm going. Patricia is expecting me."

"It's after midnight! Where are you going *now?*"

"There's a taxi on its way. I'm going to stay in the hotel near the station, so I can catch the early train out of this *God Forsaken* city."

"No, honey. Stay, we can talk about this."

She looked around her, staring at the black and white pictures on the wall of her and her husband that taken throughout the years. They were never blessed with children and after a few failed attempts, Sam had persuaded her into believing that they didn't need to have children to live a happy life together. He had made her give up her dream, and she finally realized that his reasons were purely selfish. He lived for his job, and she was just his housekeeper.

A car horn sounded in the driveway. She picked up a suitcase in each hand and asked her husband to move out of her way. "You may think I'm leaving because I don't love you anymore. The truth is, I do love you. I just don't think you love me."

"What!? Don't be crazy, honey! Of course, I love you!"

"Do you?"

"Yes," he said, turning his head towards the front door where a knock dotted the ensuing silence.

"Let him in, Sam."

"Wait..."

"Please, let him in... if you love me."

"Stop saying that! What makes you think that I don't love you?"

Ignoring him, she marched past him and pushed him out of the way, which was easy to do considering he was barely able to stand. She opened the door to the taxi driver who wordlessly took the two suitcases from her hands. Walking across the foyer, she picked up the rest of her luggage. "Don't forget to eat," she told him in farewell. "And thank you."

"Thank you for what?" he said, leaning against the wall in a half-crouched position.

"For forgetting my birthday yesterday. It helped me make my decision today. We are a product of our choices Sam, and I refuse to play the victim any longer. Good-bye." She leaned forward, kissed him on the cheek, opened the door, and left.

Shocked, Valetti fell the rest of the way to the floor. His wife was gone, and he was alone and just like the Christmas tree that sat in their living room, the lights were dimmed – in his heart.

Twenty-One

Michael was exhausted. It took longer than usual to close the restaurant. Some patrons refused to leave until they savoured every last drop in their glass. One man was intent in winning back his money at pool if it took him all night. Finally, Michael shut off the music, turned up the house lights, and bellowed to them that it was last call, like it, or not.

On the drive home, he thought about the one-eyed man named Sam. Something wasn't right about him and it wasn't just the fact that he was a cop who liked his Scotch. The way he called him "Michael", as if he knew him, made no sense. Most patrons at the restaurant called him Mr. Rossi. Only his regulars and good friends called him "Michael" or "Mike".

On the road before him, he saw a carousel spinning. Michael scrunched his eyes closed and then opened them again, but it was still there, taunting him. The reference Sam made to ride had unnerved him. It was like an inside joke that Michael failed to understand.

Reaching his house, he pulled into the driveway and turned off the engine. He sat in the car for a few minutes, finishing the last of his smoke and listening to the rest of *Stairway to Heaven.*

He couldn't wait to kiss Maria and then throw himself on the bed next to Nicole. He opened his car door and walked up the staircase and even outside, a door in his way, he could hear the cries coming from inside the house. Frantic, he put the keys in the lock, but they fell from his trembling hands.

He cursed, screamed Nicole's name, and picked them up again. After what felt like minutes, he managed to open the door and swung it open so that it hit the back wall and made the window in the door shake.

The sound of the baby's wails was deafening. His boots covered in snow, he took the stairs two at a time, tripping halfway up. The house was dark, and he followed the moonlight to Maria's room where she stood in her crib, crying, and screaming.

Picking her up, he tried to console her. "Shh, daddy's here, shh…"

He bounced her up and down, and kissed her face, until finally, she grew quiet, and his heart almost burst out of his chest when she smiled at him.

"Where's mommy? Eh? Should we go find mommy?"

He held the baby tight against his chest where she played with the buttons of his winter coat.

"Nic!"

He walked to their bedroom, but the bed was still made.

"Nic!" he called again.

He descended the stairs carefully so as not to slip on the melting snow with the baby in his arms and turned on the lamp on the small table that held the telephone.

Finally, he found his wife on the couch where she slept soundly, oblivious to all the noise. Sitting next to her, he shook her by the shoulder.

"Nicole. Wake up, baby."

Her eyes fluttered until they opened and at the sight of her husband holding Maria, she shot up as if electrified.

"What's going on? What time is it!?"

"It's almost one. I just got home. Maria was screaming. What happened, Nic?"

"Oh, God… give her to me!" she begged, her arms outstretched. "Is she okay?"

"Yeah, I think so. What the hell happened?"

Nicole's tears fell onto the baby's head. Michael stood and walked over to close the front door, securing it with the deadbolt. He walked back to the couch and sat next to his wife, urging her to talk to him.

"I...fell asleep."

Michael looked at the coffee table where the baby monitor sat. He picked it up to make sure that it was working properly, and that the volume was up. It was in the same working condition as it always was. Placing it back on the table, he took Nicole's hand.

"I think she's hungry."

"Yes, I missed feeding time." Turning to the baby, she whispered, "I'm sorry. I'm so sorry. Let's go eat, okay?"

Michael got up and extended his hand, helping Nicole to her feet. She teetered unsteadily. He watched as she went to the kitchen and placed the baby in her highchair, opened a cupboard, and grabbed a can of formula.

Worried, Michael walked over to her and pulled her into a hug. "Are you okay?"

Nicole pulled away from him and slammed the can that she was holding on the kitchen counter. "No, Michael. No, I'm not okay."

"What's going on!? Talk to me!"

The cupboard still open, Nicole sighed and pulled the bottle of pre-natal vitamins down, setting it on the counter. Michael stared at it, confused.

"I don't get it."

Ashamed, she didn't look at him when she told him, "They're not vitamins."

"What do you mean?"

"Open it."

Opening the bottle, he poured a few pills into his hand.

"They're anti-depressants," she told him.

"For what?"

"Edward thinks... he thinks I have something called G.A.D."

"What's that?"

Nicole was finished preparing the bottle and she took

Maria from her highchair and walked wordlessly out of the kitchen. Michael slid the pills back in the bottle he was holding and placed it in the pocket of his winter coat and followed her. He sat in the armchair next to the couch where Nicole sat feeding the baby.

"Tell me, Nic."

"It's short term for Generalized Anxiety Disorder. The pills are supposed to help but I... took more than I should have today."

"Anxiety disorder?"

"To help me stop worrying."

Dumbfounded, he ran his fingers through his hair and sat back in the chair. He noticed the purple bruises underneath his wife's eyes and the tears that were still welled in them. "Everyone worries, baby."

"Not like me."

"What's different about you?"

"Without the pills, I'd rather not think at all. The blackness would be friendlier."

Her words resonated something dark and morbid, and the hairs on his arms stood on end. He sat on the edge of the chair, motioning with his hands. "What are you trying to say? Were you trying to... kill yourself?"

"No!" she told him, quickly. Turning back to the baby, she said, "But I *was* trying to forget."

"How many did you take, Nic?"

"Six."

"How many are you supposed to take?"

"One, as needed. Not to exceed two a day."

Michael stood, towering over her. "Two? *Two!?* And you took six? What were you thinking baby? You could have seriously hurt yourself... and Maria."

"I know..." she whispered.

He knelt beside her and put his head in her lap. Looking up at her, he pleaded, "Never again. Okay?"

"I can't promise you that, Michael."

"What do you mean?" he asked, shooting his head up.

"I'll go crazy. I just know it."

"Jesus, Nic..." he said, standing again. Reaching into his pocket, he produced the bottle. "Are these the only ones?"

She looked at it, suddenly frightened. "Yes. Please give it to me," she told him, pushing her free hand towards him.

"No," he said, placing it back in his coat pocket.

"Michael."

"Beg all you want, Nic, you're not getting them back."

"Those were prescribed to me!"

The baby cried underneath her bottle at the sound of her mother yelling.

"And you obviously can't handle them!" Michael yelled back.

"Don't talk to me as if I'm a child."

"In my opinion," he told her, lighting a smoke from the package that sat on the coffee table, "you're acting like one."

"You're an asshole."

Infuriated, he walked over to the mantel and leaned on it. "Nice mouth."

"You don't get it. You don't understand that it's a mental illness."

"Well, you weren't *mental* a few weeks ago, so..." The tip of his cigarette glowed, and he puffed on the smoke like an addict.

"So what? So what, Michael? What does that mean? Are you making light of how I feel?"

He didn't answer her. She stared at him in silence until she got up and walked over to the staircase, the baby on one hip

"Be careful, the stairs are wet."

"You're worried about the stairs? I'm glad I can count on you. I'm glad I can tell you everything and still feel like shit, afterwards." Sarcasm dripped from her lips.

Marching over to where she was standing, he held the banister with one hand and looked up at her. "You *can* tell me anything. I *want* you to tell me *everything*. But these," he said, rattling the bottle in his pocket, "are not welcome in my home."

Looking down at him, she shook her head. "So what do you want me to do, then?"

"When you're worried? Talk to me."

"You think it's that simple, or is your head really that big?"

Without uttering another word, she walked the rest of the way up the stairs. Michael stood frozen in place. He wondered if she had heard of the third murder in the city. He heard the report himself on the ride home, swearing and cursing at the innocent reporter whose job it was to break the news. He couldn't blame Nicole for worrying with a sick bastard roaming the streets, but it was more than that. His wife felt like she was losing her mind, and nothing could help her. Nothing, except a little white pill.

She was right. He didn't get it. The concept was foreign to him. In his world, there was nothing a good yelling match and a bottle of wine couldn't fix. He had once witnessed his own father make a million dollar deal that way. When he bought the restaurant, it was from a long-time friend, Luigi. The man had brought the paperwork with him to the Rossi household and Peter Rossi looked it over and then peered at the man over his reading glasses.

"*What's this?*"

"*What?*"

"*This stipulation.*"

"*It's normal legal stuff, Pete.*"

"*You want me to just hand the place back to you if I should die? What about my son?*"

"*He's a child.*"

"*He won't be a child forever! I'm paying you for the place and you are a crook!*"

"*It's for security. It won't happen.*"

"*Security? Security for who? There's nothing normal about this stipulation. You just want to enjoy the fruits of my labour without lifting a damn finger!*"

"*Calm down. Have some wine.*"

The two men went at it for hours while Michael's mother wrung her hands nervously as she listened from the other room. After some hefty shots to the ego and multiple Italian swear words, the two men shook hands over their last glass of wine. Luigi left for Italy the next day – the stipulation *forever erased from the paperwork.*

Michael took off his coat and hung it on the hall tree. Remembering, he grabbed the bottle of medication from the pocket and stuffed it in his jeans. He loved his wife more than he loved life itself, but he was not going to watch her drug herself to death. Taking off his boots, he turned off the lamp and walked up the stairs, mentally and physically drained.

~

Michael tossed and turned in his sleep. Sweat drenched the sheets beneath him. He was dreaming that he was at work, behind the bar:

The one-eyed man was the only person in the place. He drank swiftly from his endless glass of Scotch. The patch over his eye covered half his face. He was asking Michael strange questions that he couldn't answer. Michael's throat was closed. The man's features grew more comical. It started with his lips as they stretched into a long thin line reminiscent of The Joker *from the comic book. Then his forehead grew so that his one eyebrow sat far above his one good eye. The questions continued and became more and more deranged.*

"*Well, Michael? Do you like it warm or cold?*" he asked him, *pulling a flask from his sport coat and spilling blood all over the bar.*

"*Warm,*" Michael told him telepathically.

"*Me too,*" the one-eyed man replied.

The Scotch in his glass never dissipated but he asked him anyway, "*How many have I had, Michael?*"

Michael slammed his fist on the bar eight times.

"*That many, eh?*"

Again, Michael answered him telepathically, "Yes."

The man laughed until his mouth was in the shape of an "O" and as big as an orange. Michael watched in horror as the faces he saw in there swirled around and around, their own mouths open in a silent scream.

Suddenly, the one-eyed man's features went back to normal and Michael found his voice again. "Eight," he repeated, out loud this time. "And countin'."

He opened his eyes feeling bile rise to his throat. Michael jumped from bed and ran down the hallway, vomiting in the toilet until his throat felt raw. He spat, and coughed, until there was nothing left inside of him. He sat on the edge of the bathtub, his head in his hands, and as the image became clearer and clearer, he scrunched his fingers in his hair and pulled at it. The image was a photographic masterpiece and earned National recognition. It was signed: Eric Summers.

Rising to his feet, he stared at himself in the mirror. His eyes were hard. The carousel materialized again and then he saw Nicole and he heard her words from earlier in the night and this time, they made sense. He was going to help his wife if it killed him. He had a choice to make, and as he stared at the carousel, spinning endlessly in a realm far removed from his own, he realized that his only choice was to jump on, and enjoy the ride.

Twenty-Two

"Get in here, Jacob."

Jacob put the receiver down and walked to Michael's office and let himself in. He stood in front of the desk, swallowing hard. Michael never called him by his true name. It was always "Kid".

"Is this about that underage guy drinking Blue, Mike? Because if it is, Mo served him, not me."

"Sit down."

Jacob sat in the leather chair across from his boss who looked like the devil had jumped inside him. Michael had left home before sunrise. Nicole had slept with her back to him all night. He had kissed her in her hair, checked on the baby, and made his way to *Michael's Place* like a thief in the night. A snowplow was his only companion on the road and the driver had greeted him by raising a bottle in his direction that hid underneath a brown paper bag. When he walked into the restaurant, he could almost hear the echoes of last night's dinner service as if a phantom party was still taking place.

Jacob noticed several empty espresso cups that were stacked high on his desk. "How long you been here?"

"Since dawn."

"Christ. Couldn't sleep or what? What's up?"

"I need you to help me."

Breathing a slight sigh of relief, he told him, "Sure. Anything you need, boss."

"I'm serious kid. I know you have a tendency to open your mouth."

Insulted, Jacob asked him, "Who told you that?"

"Your wife."

"She did?"

"Yeah. Are you okay to help me or what?"

"Yeah," he told Mike, picturing his wife, Kim, over his knee. "Fill me in."

Michael lit a smoke and pushed the pack in Jacob's direction.

"Trying to quit again."

"That guy from yesterday... I have a bad feeling about him."

"The one with the eye patch?"

"Yeah."

"Why?"

"He mentioned the carousel."

Mike's story was well known to everyone. It was all over the news and late one night, a few weeks after Nicole killed Stevie, Mike and Nicole opened their hearts to Jacob and his wife, as if telling someone everything would make it all go away.

"That's weird," Jacob told him.

"You catch on fast, kid."

"You said he's a cop, though."

"So?"

"He must know what happened to you."

"Then why wouldn't he say so? He pretends he has no clue who I am. He talked about my scars as if he didn't know a thing about them."

"I changed my mind," Jacob said, pulling a smoke from the pack and lighting it. Inhaling, he asked, "You got a bad vibe from him?"

"That's why we're here."

"What are you planning?"

"Get more out of him. I need to get him alone and I need to get him drunk, and..." Mike said, trailing off and opening his top desk drawer. "I need to feed him these." He placed the bottle of pre-natals in front of his friend who stared at it curiously.

"They're not vitamins," Mike finished.

"What are they?"

"Anti-depressants."

"Yours?"

"They're Nicole's."

Jacob nodded in understanding. His friend would step in front of a speeding train for his wife. He could see the determined look in Michael's eyes and once he had a plan, nothing could stop him from executing it. True love doesn't have a boundary, nor does it have an expiry date.

"What do you need from me?"

Crushing out his smoke, Michael told him, "I need to close the restaurant tomorrow afternoon."

"What? We're booked solid."

"Call everyone you can and reschedule their reservation. I'll deal with the rest. I also need you to inform all the staff. Tell them they'll still get paid for their shift."

"I can do that."

"I'll need something else. You up for it?"

"I guess it depends on what *it* is."

"I'm sure it's illegal, but if it works, it'll be worth it."

Jacob swore and stood to walk in a circle around his chair and then sat down again, "Lay it on me."

"I need two Sambuca bottles, three quarters full. You're going to dump one of them and fill it with water instead. In the other one, you're going to put some of these pills in it. Crush them up good."

"That's the illegal part."

"Yeah. But I've seen the guy drink, and straight alcohol isn't going to cut it. Even if I do it myself, you would sort of be in trouble just for hearing the plan."

Jacob sucked in air and held it before expelling it in one long puff. "Kim might murder me but I'm here for you, Mike. I'll do it."

"Just don't tell her."

"What about Mo? He'll wonder what the hell is going on.

Not to mention Mario might have a heart attack."

"Let me deal with them. Just be absolutely sure that you know which Sambuca bottle is which."

"I'll mark it with a pen."

"Good. I'll make this up to you, kid," Mike told him, extending his hand.

Jacob shook it. "I feel a bit like a *Hardy Boy*."

"You look like one, too," Michael told him, smirking.

Jacob got up to leave and then asked, "When?"

"I'll let you know. Shut the door, kid."

After Jacob was gone, Michael looked at his wristwatch. It was half past nine. Picking up his phone, he turned the rotary dial to zero.

"Operator, how may I help you?"

"Please connect me to the Ottawa Police Station."

"Is this an emergency?"

"No."

"One moment, sir."

A few seconds later, a woman at the station answered sounding bored. "Ottawa Police how may I direct your call?"

"Hi. I have a bit of a dilemma, actually."

"If a crime is in progress…"

"Not a crime. Last night I had a flat tire and a man helped me. He mentioned he was an officer and that his name is Sam. I wasn't able to thank him properly and I wondered if you could put me through. I just don't know what his last name is."

Michael played with the unlit smoke he held between his fingers and waited.

"Can you describe the man, sir?"

"He wears an eye patch."

"That's Detective Sam Valetti. One moment, please."

He's a *detective*.

"Valetti."

"Good morning, Sam."

"Who is this?"

"Michael. From the restaurant."

"Did I forget something?"

"No."

"Then to what do I owe the pleasure, Michael?" In the light of day and sober, the man sounded almost *friendly.*

"I'd like to extend a personal invitation. To lunch tomorrow."

Michael could hear Valetti incessantly dropping a paperclip on his desk. "In case you haven't noticed, this city has gone to hell, and I have several murder investigations to solve."

Michael thought fast, "But you have to eat, don't you? I invited the Mayor. Besides, I still owe you one."

There was a long pause and Michael felt the sweat form on his upper lip.

"What time?"

"Noon, sharp."

"I'm touched that you would think of me. Please accept my R.S.V.P. in the affirmative. I have Goddamn work to do, now. See you tomorrow."

The men hung up. Mike pressed his fingertips together and stared into space. There was no turning back, and that idea both excited him and made him want to hide. Valetti could be unstable but then again, he had dealt with an unstable psychopath in his past. He was well versed in entertaining mad men. Lunch tomorrow should be a piece of cake.

Twenty-Three

"What are those for?"

At home, Michael stood in the doorway of the kitchen watching Nicole make dinner. She moved slowly and there was no bounce in her step. Her long, dark, hair was up in a ponytail, and she wore her velvet burgundy track suit. She was as pale as a ghost.

Michael moved forward and placed the bouquet of red roses on the kitchen island. "You gotta give a guy a break, baby. You gotta forgive me."

"Are you apologizing, Michael? For what? For being an ass, or for making me feel two inches tall?"

She started to walk away from him, but he grabbed her upper arm and held it firmly. "I'm sorry for everything." Words failed him, but his eyes were pleading with her. "Say you forgive me."

She scrutinized the look in his eyes, and they held more sincerity than an innocent man in court with his hand on the Bible. She sighed and leaned into him. He held her and ran his hands up and down her back and spoke into her ear, "Nothing matters more to me than seeing you happy. You're right. I was being an ass. I was just… scared to see you that way."

His hands continued to explore her body. He wanted to touch all of her and make sure she was whole.

"I'm sorry, too. I should have told you about the pills as soon as I got them."

"Yeah, you should have."

"Did you hear?" she asked him, speaking next to his heart.

"What, baby?"

"The young girl. The third victim."

Letting her go, he leaned on the island with one hand. "I heard."

Nicole turned towards the cutting board in front of her and picked up a potato to peel it.

"Give it to me. I'll finish dinner. Go rest."

"I'm not an invalid, Michael."

"I know that. I know. I just want to help."

Relenting, she handed him the knife and walked over to the kitchen table and sat down. Her fingers lingered on her empty coffee mug. "What are we going to do?"

"About the murders?"

"Yeah."

Kill the son-of-a-bitch who's responsible, he wanted to tell her. "There's not much we can do."

"I can't take this. I need to do something, Michael. I'm tired of feeling helpless and scared. *I'm tired of living with myself!*"

He put the knife down and walked over to her. Pulling out a chair, he sat across from her, and squeezed her hand. "What do you mean?"

"Maybe… maybe I should go back to work for Cathy. Kim might watch Maria. I can't just sit around and do nothing."

"I don't think that's a good idea," he said, careful to keep his tone neutral.

"Why not?"

"I'll worry too much about you."

"I'll come with you, then. I'll help out at the restaurant."

"Yeah. Yeah, baby. That's a great idea."

"It is?"

"Yeah, it is. Next week," he said. Getting up, he walked to the stove and turned the gas on underneath a pot of water meant for the potatoes.

"What's wrong with tomorrow?"

"Tomorrow's no good," he said, his back to her.

"Why not? We're always busy as hell in December."

Standing back in front of his chair and leaning on it, he spoke his first lie, "There's a private party tomorrow. The restaurant's closed."

"Oh. Who?"

"I don't know. Some women's club. Mo took the booking."

"Well, why can't I help with the party?"

Walking away, his fingers in his hair, he told her, "It's not a big party."

"Then why close the restaurant?"

"Dammit, Nic!" he said, turning to face her and slamming his palm on the kitchen island.

"What? What did I say?"

"Nothing," he quickly said, changing his tune. "Nothing, baby. I'm sorry. My nerves are shot, that's all."

He took an open bottle of wine that sat in front of him and pulled at the cork. Grabbing a glass from the cupboard he asked Nicole if she wanted one.

"No."

"Don't be mad, Nic."

"I'm not mad but you're acting strange, you know that?"

"Yeah. Like I said, my nerves... just come to the restaurant next week, okay?"

"Okay, okay."

They grew silent and Nicole watched him as he worked peeling the potatoes, drinking often from his glass. It was snowing outside, and she turned towards the window, entranced with the way it fell underneath the streetlights. She wanted to tell him that she knew he was lying and that there was a reason that he didn't want her at the restaurant tomorrow. She wanted to know what that reason was, but every time she looked at him, a deeper frown invaded his face – one that invited others to stay away from him. She's seen that frown before. He wore the same one in the middle of his dance with Stevie Phelps on the carousel, seconds before Stevie lit the match, engulfing him in flames. The fire still burned.

Twenty-Four

The Next Day

At home, Jacob dusted the snow off his coat and hung it in the hallway closet. He was a nervous wreck. He was thinking of Mike and his self-imposed mission. Michael's passion often took him to dangerous places, and he wanted to do more to help his friend, but his hands were tied. He looked at his watch obsessively, and after mindlessly driving around town, he decided to just go home where Mike could call him if he needed him.

Earlier, he had double, and triple checked the Sambuca bottles. As he crushed up the anti-depressants, he felt like a medieval chemist or someone out of Shakespeare and the tragedy was materializing on the stage of life. He was not a religious man, but he asked upon a higher power to keep an eye out. Michael was one of the good ones, and he deserved to be at peace.

In the living room, he found Kim lying on the couch on her belly, engrossed in a paperback. He sneaked up on her and spanked her once, hard. Flipping over, she sat up and clutched at her heart.

"Jesus, what are you doing home?"

"Move over," he said, pushing at her legs. He sat down next to her and grasped her head, kissing her passionately. Still holding her by the nape of her neck, he asked her, "Did you tell Mike that I can't keep a secret?"

"So? You can't!" Kim said, freeing herself.

"He's my boss, honey."

"He's also your friend. You don't think he knows you by now? And what are you doing home?"

"Private party. Restaurant's closed."

"He didn't need you?"

"That's what he said."

"Well, this is great. You can help me wrap the boys' gifts before they get home from school."

She stood, pulling her sweater down and Jacob grabbed her, making her sit next to him again.

"What?"

"I love you, you know."

"All right. Spill it, mister," she said through the slits in her eyes.

"What are you talking about?"

"It's eleven in the morning, and you're home from work because of some mysterious party, and now you're wearing that same look that you did when we first met."

"What look is that?"

"The puppy-dog look!"

"So, in other words, I can't tell you that I love you or you'll get suspicious?"

"Argh! You can drive me nuts, sometimes!"

The sound of a baby crying brought Kim to her feet again.

"What the hell is that?"

"Not what. Who. And it's Maria."

She walked out of the room and into the spare bedroom where her parents stayed every Summer for a month. They were retired Professors and the rest of the year, they sojourned to exotic places, living the hell out of life.

Jacob followed her, firing questions at her. "When did she get here?"

"About an hour ago. Why?"

"Where's Nic?"

"She said she wanted to go Christmas shopping."

Kim lifted the baby from the crib and held her in the crook of her arm, staring lovingly into her eyes.

"Are you sure?"

"About what?" she asked, turning to her husband.

"That's she's Christmas shopping!"

"Of course, I'm sure! Do you think I've gone deaf now, too? Hold her for a second, would you?"

Kim handed him the baby and he raised her above his head, making her laugh her tiny laugh. He placed her on his hip and watched as Kim went over to the change table, prepping a new diaper.

"Why didn't she just take the kid with her?"

"God, almighty, Jacob, what's with all the questions? She'll get her shopping done in half the time if she's alone." She stared at him for a full minute, her lips slightly curled.

"What? What are you staring at?"

"Do you know how damn sexy you look with that baby on your hip?"

"Oh, yeah?"

"Uh-huh."

Kim took Maria and lied her down on the change table. She felt Jacob's arms around her waist and his nose in her hair. Letting her go, he stood in the threshold of the doorway and watched her.

"Oh, Nic invited us over on Boxing Day."

"That was nice. Are we going?"

"Of course!"

"Do we need to bring anything?"

"Nope. I'll buy them a gift though…." she said, trailing off. "Oh, yeah! I almost forgot. She wanted something else. She asked what pre-natals I used with Russ and Todd. I think they're trying again."

Jacob's face changed colour and his lips moved as if talking to himself.

"What's wrong?"

"Nothing," he said flatly.

"Are you sure?"

"Yeah. I'm going for a smoke."

"Okay."

She looked after him and then whispered to Maria in baby-talk while tickling her belly, "My husband's a strange one. Yes, he is... yes, he is..."

Jacob grabbed his coat and stood on his porch. Lighting a smoke, he puffed on it on eagerly. There was no way that Nicole could suspect what was going on at the restaurant but the fact that she mentioned the vitamins was too coincidental for his liking.

Jacob stared at the scene in front of him. Two pre-school children were frolicking in the snow in their front yard. Their mother waved at him, and he put two fingers to his forehead and nodded back his greeting.

"Stay young as long as you can," he said out loud.

He wished he could confide in Kim and take the pressure off himself, but he couldn't. He wondered if he should call Mike and tell him that Nicole wasn't home, but that might worry him into making a mistake. He even contemplated calling Mo to confess everything, but that would buy him a coffin once Mike found out. He had to keep everything to himself, and that fact gnawed at him until the smoke between his fingers burned to the nub. Keeping secrets, he realized, is for the birds.

Twenty-Five

In the light of day and empty, Michael's Place looked eerie. Mike stood behind the bar, smoking cigarettes in succession and surveying the two Sambuca bottles that Jacob had prepared. He marked the one without alcohol, with a nondescript "X" on the label, and Michael took a second swig of it just to ensure it was filled with water. He had crushed six pills and put them in the other bottle. Michael found it ironic that he used the same number of pills that Nicole said she took the night she fell into a coma-like slumber. Jacob had offered to stick around and hide in Mike's office or the kitchen, but it was too risky, and Michael sent him home where it was safe. He reminded him to keep his mouth shut, and then he also told him that should anything happen to him, that he was to tell Nicole everything.

"You're worrying me, buddy."
"Just give me your word."
"Of course. I promise."
"And you'll look after her, kid? And Maria?"
"Like family," he promised, again.

Michael looked at the neon *Budweiser* clock behind him. It was a quarter to twelve. This morning, he had held Nicole longer than usual, Maria between them. He kissed them both multiple times, and then to erase the look of concern on Nicole's face, he told her that he was craving chicken for dinner.

On the drive over, Jacob's words rang in his ears. Valetti was a cop. The kid was right. He should know who Michael is. Everyone knew who Michael and Nicole were. Their story stayed on the front page of *The Herald* for weeks, and there came a point where he banned the newspaper from his restaurant, until inevitably, a new story unfolded that would captivate the city and they were able to walk in broad daylight freely, and undisguised.

Valetti was hiding something, and like an excavator of words, Michael was ready to unearth the truth. The front door opened. The man's stomach preceded him.

Michael stood with his arms crossed, a smoke between his fingers. As Valetti approached, he looked around him at the tables that housed opened bottles of wine and fresh bread. Mike and Jacob had staged the place to hopefully fool the man whose job it was to solve mysteries. Music played in the background to hide the fact that there was no noise was coming from the kitchen, and fake gifts sat in one corner of the bar.

Valetti made his way across the dining room to where Michael was standing and pulled out a bar stool.

"Welcome."

"Am I early?"

"Right on time. The Mayor had to cancel. He sends his regards," he told him, pouring him a shot of Sambuca without asking if he wanted it. He slid the glass in front of the man who held it between two fingers.

Out of Valetti's line of vision, Michael pushed the bottle of alcohol underneath the bar to the far right.

"What are the tables for? Who else did you invite?"

"No one else. Staff party. Later this afternoon."

Valetti nodded and lifted his glass. The glass hovered in midair.

"I don't like to drink alone, Michael."

"Right."

Reaching underneath the counter to his left, Michael pulled out the bottle filled with water and poured himself a shot. He raised it in Valetti's direction and cheered him in the traditional Italian way, "Salute."

"Salute."

Michael threw his head back and downed the drink, smacking his lips as if it was real alcohol. He left Valetti sitting alone, made his way to the kitchen, and grabbed an antipasto plate that Jacob had prepared. Remembering a napkin, cutlery, and a small plate, he walked back out to the dining room and placed the food in front of the detective who dug in plucking a goat-cheese stuffed pepper off the plate, along with a few olives, slices of prosciutto, and some fresh bread.

"You're not eating?"

"Nah. Celebrating."

"What's the occasion?"

"My wife just found out she's pregnant again," Michael said, gagging on his lie.

"Tanti auguri."

"Thanks," Michael told him, filling his shot glass again and drinking it in one gulp.

"Don't mind if I join you."

Valetti pushed his shot glass forward and Michael reached underneath the bar. The food was meant to distract him so that he wouldn't be watching Michael too closely. As the man tore into his bread, Michael took his shot glass and replaced it with a rock glass he had prepared earlier. Before pouring, he asked him, "Neat?"

"Yeah."

Michael nodded and poured a double into the glass, no ice.

"A double sounds good," Mike said.

He walked to where the clean glasses were stacked, buying himself time. The more Valetti drank, the easier it would be to keep up the ruse of the two Sambuca bottles. He returned with the clean glass, added two ice cubes, and poured from the bottle marked with an X.

"Mind if I smoke while you eat?"

"Be my guest. So, Michael," Valetti said, spitting a little, "what would you like to talk about?"

"Talk?"

"Since we have the place to ourselves."

Wordlessly, Michael walked around the bar and to the front door where he turned the lock. Back at the bar, he told

Valetti, "Forgot to lock the door."

"I noticed. So? Do you want to talk about why we're here?"

"Just sharing in the Christmas spirit. And your free lunch," Mike added, raising his glass to his lips.

"I see."

Valetti emptied his own glass and pushed it forward. He clapped his hands together to make the breadcrumbs fall from them and waited while Michael poured.

"Do you know what I hate?"

"What do you hate?"

"Those people who win the lottery on the first ticket they ever bought. Doesn't seem fair, does it, Michael?"

The air grew thick. Michael placed one foot on the pipe beneath him and leaned with his elbow on his knee. "Life isn't fair."

"That's a profound statement coming from someone so young," Valetti said, raising his eyebrows. "What makes you say that?"

"Seen my share of injustices. Not really Christmas talk, is it?"

"Would you rather we sing Christmas carols?"

Michael smirked at the man. Standing straight again, he asked him, "How's the food?"

"It'll pass. What happened to the Mayor?" Sam asked him, signaling that he wanted another drink.

"Don't know. Some Christmas Parade."

"That's strange."

"Why is that strange? He's the Mayor."

"Because I don't know of any parades in town today," he told him, his glass poised near his lips.

Michael cleared his throat and cracked his knuckles. "Well, that's what he said."

"Huh. The Mayor's an asshole, you know."

"Not a friend of yours, then?"

"I don't make friends with pussies. Had him over to my house for dinner, once. The jerk left right after dinner. Wife hadn't even served dessert yet. She worked all day on that damn Tiramisu. Being ungrateful is a terrible sin, don't you think? Which of the Seven Deadly Sins is your favourite?"

Sweat beaded Michael's forehead but he placated the man, "Hadn't thought about it," he told him, lighting another cigarette.

"You've never thought about it? Well, I think Sloth is a good one. There's nothing more deranged than a man who won't use his God-given limbs for the better good. A man has a duty... an obligation."

"What might that be?"

"Now you're just playing with me, aren't you, Michael? You know damn well what man's duty is," he said, leaning back in his chair, his hands on his belly. "Enough about me, though. Tell me about you."

"What do you want to know?"

"Are you a proud man? Humble? What if this place burned down tomorrow? Would it bother you?"

Like the previous time, Valetti was talking gibberish. Michael could sense an evil energy coming from the man, like an angry spirit visiting a seance.

"It could always be rebuilt. Isn't Pride one of the Seven?"

"You're a good student, Michael. Glad to see you're paying attention."

They remained quiet, staring at each other. Michael poured himself another fake drink and clinked his glass against Valetti's. He feigned a cough as it went down his throat.

"It is a nice restaurant, by the way."

Michael kept his gratitude to himself. "What about your work?"

"What about it?"

"It must be difficult. Death, murder."

"Someone's gotta do it," Valetti said, seriously. "I've had many vocations in my life. Mechanic, appliance repairman. I even installed security systems for a spell."

"Jack of all trades?"

"A man has to do what a man has to do. Don't you agree, Michael?"

"For his family."

"For *himself*."

The radio announcer was reporting an expected ten centimetres for the morning.

"The snow. Now that's pure," Valetti said dreamily. He grew pensive for a moment and then added. "Ask me again."

"Ask you what again?"

"What happened to my eye."

"What happened?"

Valetti paused in the same manner Michael had seen a hundred times before. He was feeling the effects of the alcohol, and the pills were speeding up the process. Valetti was taking too long to find his words and his one eyelid drooped slightly.

"Do you believe in God, Michael?"

"Don't want to talk about it?"

"Answer the question."

"Yeah," Michael crooked one thumb in his belt, a smoke dangling between his lips.

"That's what she said, too."

"Who?"

Valetti downed the Sambuca he was still holding. He slammed the glass on the bar and tapped his fingers on it, "Another."

Michael poured the drink and then watched as the detective moved forward in his chair as if to whisper a secret. His face was blotched red, and purple veins ran down his cheeks like tributaries.

"The *Goddamn* whore who did this to me," he said, sitting back. "The boys at the precinct think I lost it in a street-fight. Wife, too. She pleaded, of course, but I punished her for what she did. At the end of it all, I stuck a hundred-dollar bill in her empty eye socket. Still had to pay the slut."

Michael stared at him and bit at the inside of his cheek to silence himself. He pulled the smoke from his lips and put it out in an ashtray that sat on the bar, feeling a dampness in his armpits.

"What's wrong, Michael."

"Never said anything was wrong."

"You're judging me."

"What makes you say that?"

"The look in your eye. Speaking of which, do you want to see a bar trick?"

Valetti stood next to his chair. Michael crooked his thumb deeper in his belt nervously, unsure of the man's next move.

Taking his glass, Valetti put it underneath him and lifted his eye patch. The sound of something falling in his drink caused the two men to lock eyes. The detective grinned, proud of himself, and picking up his glass, he handed it to his host.

Michael's hands trembled as he took it. A flash of red crossed his vision – the blood he saw in his dream. He stared into it, unsure of what he was seeing. It floated in the beverage like an olive in a martini, but it was brown, and shrivelled like a raisin with stringy bits surrounding it.

"Jesus *Christ!*"

Michael let go of the glass so that it spilled over the bar and a human eyeball rolled forward straight towards him. He stared at it where it stopped, meeting the wood barrier of the bar.

"So, you *do* believe in God," Valetti said laughing, and sitting back down.

Slowly, Michael raised his head to look at Valetti who was casually swinging back and forth in his stool and smiling foolishly.

"You sick *fuck*."

"Maybe. But at least I'm not stupid. Why don't you pour me another drink, Michael?"

Mike stood frozen, berating himself for not putting a weapon of some sort underneath the bar. He threw a napkin over the eyeball and stepped backwards, hitting the beer fridge.

"Pour me another, Michael," Valetti repeated, offering the

same glass that had just held Stacy Rodman's eye.

Michael stepped forward and grabbed the Sambuca. His palms were sweating profusely causing the bottle to slip.

"Careful, now."

Mike caught it and raised it over the glass. The booze filled with drugs was the only thing he had to protect himself. It was liquid ammunition.

With lightning speed, Valetti gripped Michael's wrist. There was raw hunger in his eye like an exotic animal about to feed. "Funny how we've both been drinking doubles, and yet this bottle stays full."

"Let go of me," Michael said through clenched teeth. Without hesitating, Valetti let him go. He was enjoying himself and pouncing on his host had only been foreplay.

"It's you, isn't it?"

"Whatever do you mean?"

"Don't play stupid."

"I am anything but stupid, friend. Now, I urge you to take *this* bottle, and *not* the one hiding underneath the bar, and pour yourself a *Goddamn* drink."

"And if I refuse?"

Valetti patted his breast coat pocket where his gun hid underneath in his holster. "Then there'll be quite a mess to clean up before this staff party of yours," he joked, popping an olive in his mouth.

Michael's steely glare could have killed the man, but he remained calm, trying to think his way out of it. He took his glass and the unmarked bottle and poured himself a shot.

"More."

Again, Michael lifted the bottle and poured a second shot.

"More."

Finally, Michael tore the spout off the top of the bottle, lifted it to his lips and chugged from it, feeling the burn ride down his throat and into his chest.

"That's better. Now, where were we? Ah, yes. Now you

know my story. Are you going to tell me yours?"

Michael spat on the floor next to him. "Like you don't know? Eh? What was he to you, Valetti? Your little helper?"

The detective's fists clenched, and he slammed both on the bar. "You'll speak of him with *respect!*"

"I'd rather gouge my own eye out."

"That can be arranged," Valetti warned, reaching into his coat pocket. Before he could pull the knife out, the front door opened.

Michael's blood ran cold, and his heart leapt into his throat. He hadn't heard the lock turn and even if he had, it was too late. "Turn around and *get out! Now!*"

She had crashed the wrong party. Nicole stood frozen in place, confused. "What's going on?"

"Listen to me, baby. Get out, *please.*"

"Why?"

"Now, now, Michael. Don't be rude," Valetti told him wagging a finger at him. He turned to the door and spoke to Nicole as if she had just arrived for Christmas dinner. "Please, Mrs. Rossi, won't you join us?"

"Don't you talk to her! Don't you even dare look at her!"

With a roar, the detective stated the obvious, "I don't think you're in a position to make demands of me, Rossi!" Turning back to the door, he yelled to her, waving absurdly. "Over here, Mrs. Rossi!"

Nicole stood immobile. She had been worried about Michael. He had held her and Maria for far too long this morning and he wore the same frown as he had the night before. She dropped Maria off at Kim's and made her way to the restaurant, intent on speaking with him. The locked door made her even more curious, and she let herself in with her key. She hit the bullseye with her women's intuition. The scene before her made no sense and the tone in her husband's voice told her that something was seriously wrong. She dug her nails into her palm until they pierced her skin.

"Come to me, baby."

"That's right, come here."

"I... I don't know what to *do!*"

"It's okay. Come to me behind the bar."

She willed her legs to move, and she walked across the carpet. When she was a few feet away from Valetti, he stood and grabbed her arm, forcing her to sit in the bar stool next to him.

"Don't touch her!"

"What's going on!? Who is this?"

Valetti helped himself to the Sambuca bottle and then turned to Nicole whose face registered fear and anguish. "Allow me to explain, Nicole. May I call you Nicole? My name is Detective Sam Valetti and your kind husband," he said, slurring, "invited me to lunch today. Get the girl a glass, would you, Michael?"

"No!"

"Get the girl a *glass!*"

"Goddammit!"

"Just get the damn glass and stop being melodramatic."

Michael walked quickly to grab a glass and poured a tiny amount of the pill-laden booze in it and placed it in front of his wife whose eyebrows were permanently knitted.

Valetti stared at the centimetre of liquid and sighed. "So anyway, as I was saying. Your husband thinks he can do my job. He thinks he's a detective. But I can see right through him. You know that I can see right through you, right Michael?" he said, turning his head to see Michael standing there imprisoned by his own stupidity.

"What...what is he trying to figure out? I don't understand any of this!"

"Well, my dear," he said, patting her hand. "He's trying to determine if I'm the copy-cat killer."

"My God!" Instinctively, Nicole leaned backwards in her chair, making it tip. Valetti grabbed it from underneath and held her steady.

"I see you believe in God, too. How are you feeling by the way? I hear congratulations are in order."

"Baby, don't say another word. Okay? Just *don't*."

Cheerful, Valetti reached for Nicole's hair and held a few strands beneath his fingers. Michael moved forward and without looking at him, Valetti patted his breast pocket threateningly. Addressing Nicole, he told her, "Goddamn, you're pretty. My own wife left me, you know. I really did love her. She was the only one who understood me. Then she left…*stupid bitch*."

"Michael…" Nicole whimpered.

"It's okay, baby. Just be quiet."

"Oh, come on you two! This is a party!" Valetti said. He grabbed the Sambuca bottle and skipping the formality of a glass, drank from it and shoved it in Nicole's face. "Drink up, now."

She shook her head, desperate to wake from the nightmare.

"I said, *drink!*"

Mimicking her baby, she grasped it with both hands and brought it to her lips, barely sipping from it.

"Good, now pass it to this handsome devil, here."

Nicole held the bottle out in Michael's direction who drank from it and put it down, willing the deadly concoction to explode.

"My mama hated me," Valetti told them out of the blue. "I was a good kid, but she hated me anyway. Blamed me for papa dying. Said I should have watched over him. Damn horse kicked him in the head. How was I supposed to stop a horse? Nicole?"

"I… I don't know."

"Rossi?"

Michael stood quietly; his jaw locked.

"Nothing, eh? I don't get it either. So, she would lock me in the fruit cellar for days. Like solitary confinement. I think that's why I became a cop!" he told them, as if having a profound revelation. "One day, when I was old enough, I told her that I was leaving. She didn't flinch, or cry, or scream, or anything. She didn't try to stop me. Her final words to me were, '*Sei morto per me, orfano.'* Imagine that? Imagine a mother telling her only son that he was dead to her?"

Michael scanned the area around him. There was a bottle opener, a pen, and a cutting board directly in front of him, underneath the bar. It wasn't enough to drive the insanity out of the man who was casually picking at the antipasto plate that still sat on the bar. There was a fork on the plate, but it was a cocktail fork, and the tines wouldn't even break skin. He stared at his wife. Nicole looked like she was vibrating; her entire body was shaking. She was sitting close to Valetti, too close, but not close enough to grab the fork if she needed it – if it would do her any good.

"I'm sure you know what an orphan, is. Of course, you do," Valetti said, shaking his head at himself. "It means that I am dead to her, and she is dead to me. It all worked out, I suppose."

Sam stared at the bottles of liquor lined on the shelves behind Michael, counting them compulsively. He lost count and started over, and then he grew bored and turned his head left and right, admitting to his new friends, "I was never really good at math. What do you two say we play a party game, instead? Eh? Russian roulette?"

He reached into his coat pocket and instead of the gun, produced a hunting knife. He seemed to be oblivious to the cuts it was making to the skin of his stomach where the tip reached as he sat hunched over. He slammed the knife on the bar, making Nicole jump. Michael eyed it hungrily.

"Do you know the rules? I'll spin the knife and if lands on you… well, let's just say you lose. Ready?"

"Wait."

"What is it, Michael?"

"I'm just curious," he told him, his plan in place. "How many victims were yours?"

"What do you mean?"

"At Hayden's Park. How many of the seventy-three?" Michael could see the detective swaying in his chair. He had to keep him talking…and drinking. "You must be proud of the number? All that hard work. Don't you want to tell us about it?"

"Well, it was a lot of work…"

"I bet…something to toast, I bet," Michael said, sliding the bottle towards him.

"Cheers, to that! That asshole Stevie screwed up most of the time. Let you go," he said, turning to Nicole. "I told him, *'Stevie, never let them out alive'.*"

Nicole coughed on vomit, remembering the rape as if it was happening all over again. She also realized that she's been walking around for years with a target on her back. Stevie stayed in the park. Valetti was free to follow her and kill her at any time.

"What else did you tell Stevie? May I?" Michael asked, motioning towards the bottle.

"But of course! Here!"

Michael chugged from it and repeated, "What else did you tell Stevie?"

"Told the fat bastard I'd bring him food and whiskey if he helped me. Stupid cops at the precinct believed me when I told them he was gone. Left town. Told them he must have. Told them I scoured the place myself."

"Your colleagues are pretty stupid, eh?"

"You got that right, friend."

"Why did you pretend you didn't know me, Sam? When you came in complaining about the food?"

"To torture you. Why else?"

"Good one."

"I thought so. You were my most special assignment, Michael. Been keeping my one eye on you," he said, chuckling.

"And the recent murders?"

"What about 'em?"

"Why did you start killing again?"

Valetti turned to Nicole whose eyes were as wide as circles. "Is he always this dumb?" Turning back to Michael, he confessed, "I never stopped. I just started leaving the bodies around instead of hiding them. Thanks to you, *Signora*," he said, swivelling in his chair towards Nicole, "it's been back-breaking work without my sidekick. You were very, very, naughty to kill him, you know."

Michael cleared his throat loudly to get Valetti's attention back.

"Motive?"

"Motive? Isn't it obvious?"

"Explain it to me."

"Women, Michael, are the dirtiest lifeform to walk the face of God's green earth. They're whores, all of them. Including this one," he said, cocking his head towards Nicole, who leaned back in a futile attempt to escape him.

"You don't love your wife?"

"Love? It's a four-letter word, Michael. Honesty, what's the matter with you? Can't you spell? Sometimes, a man would try to play hero, like you're doing today. A *Goddamn* kid got in my way, once. That one, hurt. Poor kid…"

"Oh, God!"

"Shut up, Nic," Michael said impatiently.

Valetti's good eye sprung open, but his attention span was getting shorter, and he ignored Michael's not-so-subtle affront towards his wife.

"Can we get back to the game, please?" he asked, sighing.

Michael stared at the knife and then at Nicole who was shaking her head ever so slightly.

"Sure."

"Michael, what are you *doing!?*"

"I thought I told you to be quiet!?" Michael told her, raising his voice and winning Sam's attention.

"Well, well, well…I'm impressed, Rossi. That's the way to do it. Gotta treat them like animals."

"She just won't shut up, sometimes. Drives me crazy."

"I can relate. And I'm sorry."

"For what?"

"I thought I could see right through you. Thought you were a sissy. A pussy. Like the Goddamn mayor. I saw you all wrong. You don't even wear your ring on the right hand. Don't care much for marriage?"

"It's a Goddamn ring. Doesn't mean anything."

Valetti nodded and looked at Nicole's hand where the two-carat diamond shined brilliantly underneath the hanging lantern above her head. He let out a long whistle. "Nice rock. Can I see it?"

Nicole's chest heaved with her sobbing. She held her hand to her heart and covered it with her other hand.

"Come on, come on, hand it over. You know I'll just chop it off if you don't."

"Give him the ring."

"I am not giving him the ring!"

"Give him the *ring!*"

"Here!" she tore it off her finger and flung it towards Valetti who had to chase it down the bar. He picked it up, admired it, put it in his mouth and washed it down with Sambuca. Nicole looked at him, horrified, and even Michael's mouth fell open.

"What? What did you two think? That I wanted to sell it? I don't need money, what I *need* is another eye. Now, the game."

"Spin it," Michael told him, clenching his fist in his pocket.

Like a kid in a candy store, Valetti put his hand on the handle of the knife and spun it hard. He was literally bouncing up and down in anticipation. "This is exciting, isn't it, kids?"

Nicole saw the carousel spinning, and her hands clenched the side of the bar until her knuckles turned white. Michael watched the knife like an addicted gambler in a casino watches the little white ball. Valetti's eye stayed on it, his other hand on the Sambuca bottle. As it slowed down, the music in the restaurant died. It was then that Michael snatched at the knife, and with the strength of a thousand men, stabbed Valetti's free hand with it, making him one with the wood. Blood splattered on Nicole's face and her disgust was palpable in her scream. The psychopath yelled, and cursed, and tried to pull at the knife in his hand, laughing uncontrollably as he struggled to free himself. Ignoring Nicole's screams, Michael took the bottle of Sambuca that was filled with water, and slammed it against the bar sink, shattering it.

"Say hi to Stevie for us, would you, Sam?"

The broken end met Valetti's good eye. Michael twisted and turned the bottle, using all his force until the muscles in his bicep bulged. Michael practically sat on the bar, and even though his guest lay slumped backwards in his chair, his mouth gaped open, blood pouring from it, he asked him, "You saw right through me, eh? Can you see me now? Can you, *you sick prick!?*" Releasing the bottle, it remained embedded in the man's face.

Like in a Ghost Town Saloon, the music resumed, and *Silent Night* played in the background.

~

Michael jumped over the bar, causing Valetti to fall to the ground. The thud of his body hitting the floor made a sound that would haunt his dreams forever. He grabbed Nicole by both her arms, lifting her from her stool, and held her to his chest, feeling her heart race. She was hyperventilating and sobbing. "Don't look, baby. Don't look."

Michael spun her around so that her back was to Valetti, and gently grabbed the sides of her face. "You should have left. You should have listened to me. Are you *okay?* Are you okay, baby?"

Her mouth opened but no words escaped. She stared at her husband with a deep void in her eyes. She was in shock.

Holding her hand, they stepped around the lifeless lump on the floor, and the blood that pooled around it. In his office, he placed her in the leather chair by gently guiding her as if she were old, or sick. He leaned over her and kissed her hair, her face, and her eyelids, trying to erase the image from her mind of the man with the bottle in his face.

Walking behind his desk, he picked up the phone, his hands shaking.

"9-1-1. What is your emergency?"

Michael put his hand out and looked at it, enthralled with it. He put it in his armpit to stop it from shaking but it was no use.

"Is anyone there?"

"I…"

He stared down at himself and wiped at the blood on his shirt in quick up and down movements. He glanced at his wife, who looked small, and frail.

"What is your emergency, sir?"

"I'm at my restaurant and I…"

He gave up rubbing at the splatters of crimson and tore at his shirt so that the buttons flew across the room. Releasing his arms from it, he let it drop to the floor. He stood on it, pushing it back and forth with one foot, as if he was cleaning the hardwood.

"Sir!"

He found his voice again, just like in his dream. "My name is Michael Rossi, and I just killed The Carousel Killer."

The operator was silent for a few seconds and then told him, "Stevie Phelps is dead, sir."

"Not Phelps. Valetti. Detective Sam Valetti."

Twenty-Six

Six Months Later

Italy, 1929

The heat of the Sicilian sun was scorching. They needed water. The drought continued, and the crops suffered. Franco was in the fields with his son of ten years. The boy lazily attended to the plants that should have produced fruit for the family by now. He was an only child, and his father couldn't afford to pay the farm hands, forcing them to seek employment elsewhere, lest they starve.

"Dai, Salvatore, forza," his father encouraged him.

He hadn't eaten since yesterday around noon, and Sam felt the pain of his empty belly, as if his insides were being pulled from his throat. He was weak, and thirsty, and he cursed himself for not being strong, like his father.

He admired his father. Love was too small a word to describe Sam's feelings for his papa. It was more as if they were connected by a patriarchal umbilical cord and should the cord be severed, Sam would perish.

"I can't, papa. I'm hungry," he finally admitted.

Franco sat on the ground in the style of Indians, motioning for his son to do to the same. He took from his burlap sack, something wrapped in a handkerchief, and the boy watched, ravenous, as his father revealed two arancini. He handed one to Sam who waited for permission to eat. Tearing a small piece off the second one, he handed the rest to his son who suddenly felt like a rich man.

"Mangia."

Sam bit into the rice ball, saliva dripping down one side of his mouth. In better times, his mama would add a cube of mozzarella inside, and Sam would play a game with the ball, pulling at it ever-so-gently, so that the cheese would stretch – sometimes, at an arm's length.

His father smiled at him and ate the morsel in his hand, imagining it expanding in his stomach. It was only ten in the morning, but the sun was fierce, and Franco removed his hat and wiped at his brow with the handkerchief that held their breakfast. He looked up at the sound of horse's hooves trotting and getting closer. The Sheriff stopped short of the man, and Sam raised a hand to his forehead to clearly see him against the blinding sun. "Silenzio. Be quiet," Franco warned.

"Buongiorno," the Sheriff said, a pipe in one hand.

Franco rose to his feet. He owned the land that they were standing on, and the Sheriff was trespassing.

"What do you want?"

"You know what I want, Franco." Gunfire pierced the silence.

Sam dropped his lunch and brought his hands to his ears. He leaned to his side and pulled his knees to his chest, as if he was in bed sleeping.

"Was that necessary!? You're scaring the boy! Put the rifle away, Cristo!"

The Sheriff smirked and placed his rifle back around his neck. With the pipe between his lips, he said, "Just playing, Franco. Now, the papers."

"I told you last time! They burned in a fire!"

"I need papers," the Sherriff repeated. "The boy doesn't exist, otherwise."

Sam lied on the ground and listened quietly, pinching his own hand to see if he did, in fact, exist. He held his breath, waiting for his papa to speak. He could see that he was angry. He could tell by the way his lips pursed like he was about to spit on the Sherriff.

"You can see him, can't you?"

"Must be official. He must have papers. A date of birth. A signature from un medico, or priest."

Franco looked at his son, remembering the stormy night ten

years earlier when he had gone to feed the horses. Underneath the sound of thunder and the rain that pelted the tin roof of the barn, he could hear a baby crying. Franco thought he was losing his mind but as he searched the stable, mindful of where he was walking, he found the infant in a wicker basket, unclothed, and red-faced from wailing into the night. He and his wife bore no children of their own and as he carried the basket to the house and placed it on the kitchen table, he stood with his arm around his wife's waist and exclaimed triumphantly, "Mio figlio. My son."

Sweat poured down Franco's face. Without taking his eyes off the Sheriff, he told Sam, "Vieni qui."

Sam crawled to where his papa stood, and his father lifted him by his arm, his eyes still focused on the man on the horse.

"His name", he told the Sheriff, hanging on to Sam, "is Salvatore Valetti. Now get off my property before I shoot you dead with your own gun."

The Sheriff didn't move. He stared at them, trying to find similarities in their features, but of course, there were none.

From high above them, where he sat, he simply said, "The papers. I'll be back for the papers. Buona giornata," he finished, tipping his hat, and riding away.

As soon as the Sheriff's back was turned, Franco bent down and grasped his son by the shoulders, forcing him to face him.

"You are my son, and you always will be. Remember that. You are a Valetti! And a Valetti does not fear. Capisci, Salvatore?"

"Si, papa."

"Bravo. Andiamo. Let's go home for a while."

They walked the stretch of land to their house where Lucia Valetti waited. She looked out the window towards the fields every so often anticipating her husband's return.

His son, however, was like the animals in the barn. He wasn't hers. She wasn't his mama, and never would be. She stopped trying to explain it to her husband who beat her last time, until she was forced to stay in bed for a week. When the swelling was gone, and she was finally able to speak again, she begged his forgiveness, and he gifted it to her.

She seemed sincere. She seemed like she would start believing that Salvatore was hers. Franco even noticed her kiss the boy once, on the day they chose as his birthday, January 1st – the start of each year. She kissed the top of his head, and his face, and hugged him, and whispered something in his ear. The boy had smiled.

"Smile, or I'll bite your ear off and feed it to you, bastardo," she had told him...

Nicole tore the book from her husband's hands and threw it on the floor next to his side of the bed. The title was visible in a patch of moonlight, "Portrait of a Serial Killer – A True Crime Novel" by Eric Summers. She removed his reading glasses and leaned over him to place them on his bedside table, feeling his hand on her backside. Sitting up, she kissed him softly.

"Why are you reading that crap?" she asked him, pulling away.

Michael adjusted the pillow behind his back and looked his wife directly in her hazel eyes. "Don't know."

"Well, I'm burning it tomorrow," she whispered. "Turn off the lamp and let's get some sleep."

He reached over and extinguished the only light in the room, but he didn't lie down. The bedroom window was open, allowing an early summer breeze to wash over them and he felt cleansed by it. Michael watched the red, sheer, curtains blow in the wind, imagining himself somewhere in the Amazon Jungle, removed from society and all its deep, dark secrets. The Jungle was safer.

He felt his wife's head in his lap. He smoothed her long hair and caressed her cheek. His silence unnerved her.

"What are you thinking about?"

There were times he didn't even want to think. There were times when he wished he could euthanize his own thoughts. Right now, though, he was thinking how much he loved her. "I love you, baby."

"And I love you," she said, facing him.

Lifting her body, she kissed him, and he held her, supporting her, as she stayed locked on his lips and gently licked at them. The smooth, silk fabric of her nightgown was a barrier between him and the woman he adored. He pulled one thin strap from her shoulder and kissed the softness of her skin. She could smell his familiar scent, mixed with cologne, and she drank it in, nourishing her senses. He pulled at her other strap, and exposing her naked breasts underneath, he cupped one gently. Her hands ran through his hair, and down his neck, around his face. She held his jaw in one hand, rubbing one of her thumbs across his lips in between kisses.

"I wouldn't change anything, Nic. Nothing…" he said, suddenly.

"Michael…"

Pushing her down on her pillow, he climbed on top of her and supported himself with one hand, while the other raised her nightgown over her legs until it pooled around her waist. She bent one leg at the knee, and he put his hand on her thigh, squeezing it firmly, and then allowed his hand to discover her, feeling her back arch in response.

She prompted him quietly, by placing her own hand on his, guiding him to a place where she felt her heart beat furiously.

"Do you know how much I need you, baby? Eh?"

His body stretched over hers as he forced her right knee up to greet her left one. He made both of her legs obey him as he guided them around his back, her ankles locked.

Her breathing became irregular. She ached to have him. Grasping her wrists, he held them above her head and ravaged her neck, and then her mouth. Releasing her, their fingers clasped where their wedding ring tattoos would be forever etched as evidence of their love.

The breeze felt delicious on his back where her nails dug into his skin, signaling him to take her. He swallowed at the fresh air in the room, preparing himself for what was to come, filling his lungs, until finally, they were breathing as one entity --

because they were.

The rhythm of their bodies uniting mimicked the quiet rhythm of the baby monitor as it blinked at them from where it sat on her table. It wasn't really a blink, however. It was more like a wink.

Books by Barbara Avon

Peter Travis Love Stories:
My Love is Deep
Briana's Bistro
The Christmas Ornament
The Christmas Miracle

A Two-Part Love/Time Travel Story:
Promise Me

Romance/Suspense/Time Travel:
STATIC
Timepiece
Windfall

Romance/Thriller:
The Gift
Michael's Choice (Standalone sequel to "The Gift")
Sultry, Is the Night
A Crack in Forever (Standalone sequel to "Sultry, Is the Night")

Horror:
The Simpleton
SPEED BUMP

Psychological Horror/Thriller:
Sacrilege
Owl Eyes Motel
Revived

Paranormal Romance:
Postscript
Q.W.E.R.T.Y.
A Letter to Claudia: Sequel to Q.W.E.R.T.Y.

A Collection of Flash Fiction:
Love Bites
Love Still Bites

About the Author

Barbara Avon was born in Switzerland and immigrated to Canada when she was two years old. She grew up Italian in the Niagara Region and attended Notre Dame High School, and then Brock University. She moved to Ottawa, Ontario, in 1999 to pursue work. She has worked for two major Ottawa area magazines and is a published poet.

In 2018, she won SpillWords Author of the Month, as well as FACES Magazine "Favourite Female Author". Her work appears in various anthologies including Steering 23 Publications, Storytime for Grownups, and Beyond the Levee. In October of 2022, "Revived" was chosen as "Horror Book of the Year" by the "Feed My Reads" community.

When she's not writing, she's experimenting in the kitchen, reading, watching 1980s movies, or engaging with her peers on Twitter (@barb_avon). She lives in Ontario, Canada with her husband Danny, their tarantula Betsy, and their houseplant, "Romeo".

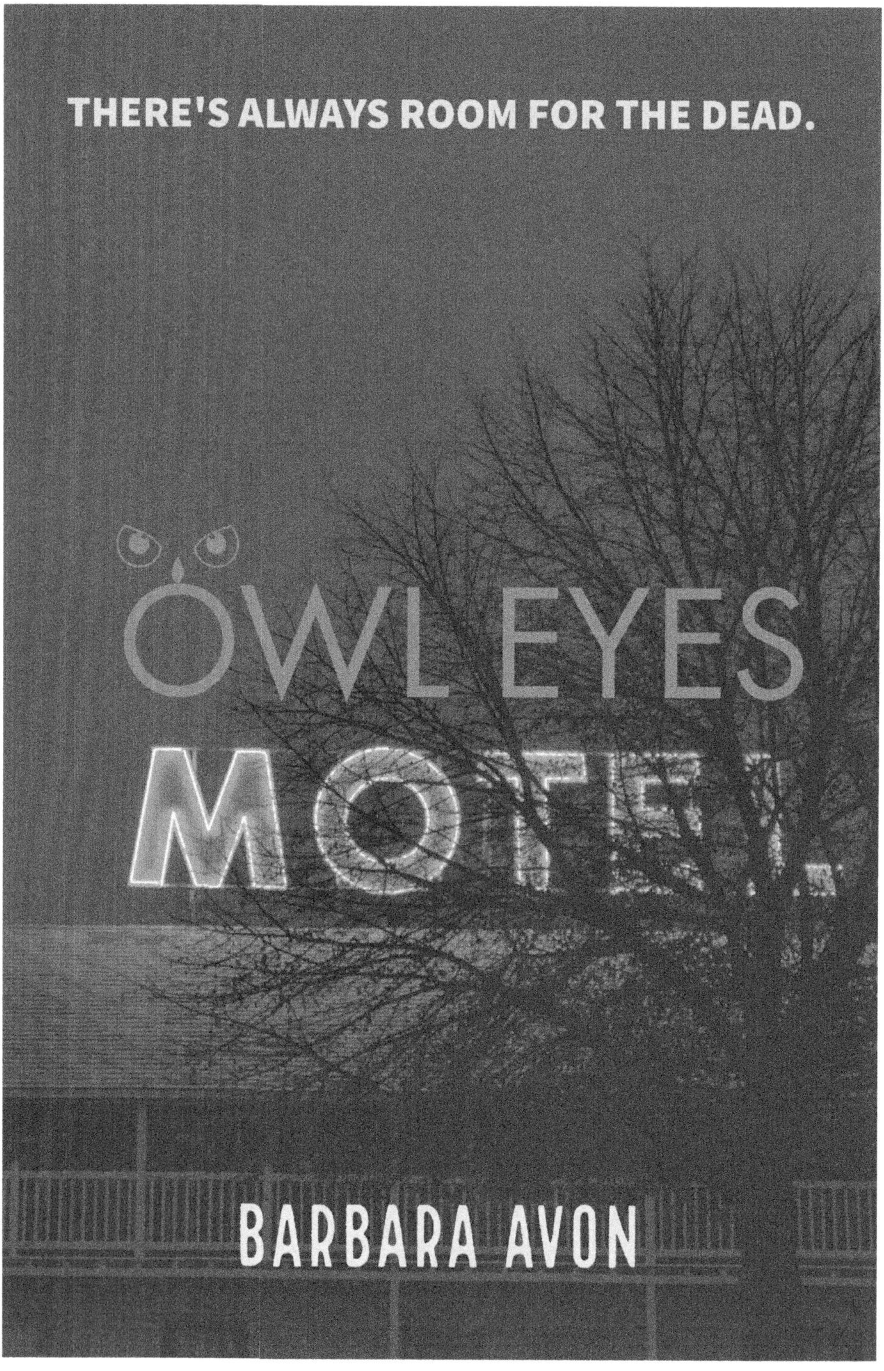
THERE'S ALWAYS ROOM FOR THE DEAD.
OWL EYES
MOTEL
BARBARA AVON

Made in the USA
Middletown, DE
08 February 2023